Huguenot Garden

Huguenot Garden

Douglas Jones

Canon Press

MOSCOW, IDAHO

Douglas Jones, *Huguenot Garden: A Children's Story of Faith*

© 1995 by Douglas M. Jones III
First published 1995. Published 1998 by Canon Press, P.O. Box
8741, Moscow, ID 83843
800-488-2034

02 01 00 99 98   9 8 7 6 5 4 3 2

Cover design by Paige Atwood Design, Moscow, ID

Printed in the United States of America

ISBN: 1-880692-21-X

For the apples of my eye (Ps. 17:8),
Amanda Renée Jones & Chelsea Albret Jones,
heirs of the covenant.
May you be mighty and fruitful warriors of the faith.

Contents

CHAPTER ONE

Friends and Enemies

The King's soldiers raced their heavy horses to the top of the hill. The group slowed for a moment and then stopped. Finally they could see the city. The soldiers stretched their necks and let their heavy arms rest by their sides. The commander spit into some grass and tried to wipe the dirt from his forehead. He smiled sharply at the city. After a moment, he slapped his horse, started down the hill, and led his soldiers quickly toward the city to do their damage.

A gentle sea-breeze cooled the faces of the twin sisters as they worked steadily in their gardens. They each wore thin, laced bonnets, as was common to little girls of long ago. The sun gently warmed their heads.

"Renée, watch out!" shouted Albret, pointing at her sister's neck.

"What? What?" cried Renée.

"A . . . a . . . a . . . bee!" squealed Albret, as she ran away in circles, almost tripping over the long thick folds of her dress.

"Oh, Albret, Mother said we shouldn't be afraid of bees. They just want to taste our flowers," said Renée with a trembling voice. Finally, she too gave way and ran squealing from the bee.

The twins met up on the other side of the yard, tumbling over each other in their silliness and giggling uncontrollably. The twins used to cry hysterically when a lone bee, or even a confused fly, had so rudely intruded upon their world.

When they stopped giggling, they immediately looked for their mother—Madame Madelaine Martineau (martin-OWE)—who was watching them out of the corner of her eye as she worked in the cooking area. She was shaking her head slowly, trying to hide her smile.

Crunch. Crunch. Crunch. The girls strained their ears toward the sound coming from around the corner of the house. *Crunch. Crunch. Crunch.* They looked at each other with wide eyes, jumped up and ran toward the sound that they recognized all too well.

"Shoo, shoo," they commanded as they ran toward the crunching. "No, no, no, no, Bouclé."

Bouclé (boo-CLAY)—or Curly—was their small lamb that had quickly invaded the girls' vegetable garden upon seeing it left unattended by its guardians.

"Get away, you sly one," said Albret, as she picked him up, leaning back as far as she could with his legs dangling above the ground as she carried him to his rope.

"These are our vegetables to tend," she said softly into Bouclé's ear.

Renée and Albret each had their own small garden plots, located on the sunny back side of the house. Last year they visited their aunt and uncle's vineyard outside the city and learned to love working with the ground and tending fruits, flowers, and vegetables. Seeing this, their father—Monsieur Paul Martineau—cleared two areas for them and started them in their own special gardens. In their first season, the twins grew onions, turnips, and peas, with each plot completely surrounded by a colorful wall of orange and yellow poppies.

This year, their Uncle Philippe (fil-EEP), the grape farmer and winemaker, brought the girls several small grapevines and taught them how to care for them. The twins were delighted, and when they prayed for their gardens with their mother, they gave special thanks for their new vines. The sisters were learning that tending a garden takes great time and care.

When they finished tying up Bouclé, Mother stepped outside, wiping her hands on the apron that hung over her beautifully round middle; she was soon to have a baby.

"Girls, I want you to go to the market with your brother and pick up more bread flour for tonight."

"Yes, Mamá," the twins said excitedly.

"May we walk through the fish market on the way back?" asked Renée.

"Yes, if you hurry," she smiled. The girls always loved the busy market with all its loud people and strange fish smells.

They moved quickly through the house on their way to the street in front. As they passed through, they each patted baby Guilliaume (gee-YOME) on his head as he sat playing on the floor with some wooden toys. Like most children of this time, Guilliaume, or "Gee Gee" as the children called him, wore a long, tan-colored robe with buttons all the way down the front.

"Dooooeeeeh!" he shouted, pointing at them, as they walked by. For some unknown reason, he always made this sound when he was pleased with something. And, while shouting it, he would point firmly, frown, and then smile at whatever pleased him. When he didn't like something or was scared, he would hold up both hands and say, "Hot!" even if the thing wasn't hot at all. He used the same word—"hot"—to describe everything that he thought was bad, whether food, loud animals, or spankings.

The twins passed through the front doorway, then turned and pushed the thick front door closed behind them.

"Hurry along," said Abraham, the eldest child in their family of five children, soon to be six. After Abraham in age was Mary, a good student and flute player, then Renée and Albret together, and finally Guilliaume, the toddler.

Abraham was fifteen years old and usually spent this time of the day training with his father in the family's fabric shop. He had short, straight, dark hair and high, suntanned cheekbones that made for a strong-looking face. Each twin gave him one hand, Abraham handed them empty flour buckets, and they all started off through the streets of their city, La Rochelle (la ro-SHELL).

Even then, La Rochelle was an old and graceful city, sitting at the end of a long bay on the coast of the country, France. The city was almost completely surrounded by tall, thick walls which, for a long time, protected the people in the city from all their enemies. From the sky, the fortress walls made the city look like a big star with many points. On the outside, the city was surrounded on one side by wide and low salt marshes and on the other side by delicious grape vineyards. Where the city touched the ocean, several stout, grey castle towers silently overlooked the city and the harbor like old, wise giants. For years, La Rochelle was home to thousands of Huguenots (HEW-ga-nots)—French Christians—like the Martineaus.

"Why did Mother send us with you?" Albret asked Abraham.

"Well, maybe she wants you to learn how to run errands," Abraham said.

"Maybe when we're older, but now we're still too small to be out here alone," said Renée as the three made their way through the narrow, crowded streets.

"Oh, I told Mother you were old enough to go out on your own," teased Abraham. The girls looked at each other with big worried eyes. Then Abraham squeezed their hands and smiled. The buckets the girls were carrying seemed to be getting heavier. Turning down one last narrow street, the children passed more houses and shops all pressed up against one another.

"Abraham, why do you think that stars . . ." started Albret, but her question was cut off by a loud noise coming up the narrow road. It sounded almost like a giant wave; some people were shouting. Just as Abraham and the twins turned around to find out what was happening, Renée was pushed to the ground by something big and brown flashing before her eyes. Albret felt the edge of a kick from something black, as the girls flew in different directions. Their buckets flew in different directions. Abraham frantically tried to pull them out of the way. Then it passed. The girls sat in the mud and grime along the side of the road, Renée on her knees and Albret on her bottom, looking confused. As they looked down the road, they saw eight or nine big horses racing down the road, carrying soldiers in armor.

"Those are . . . the King's soldiers," said Abraham in an angry tone, as he got up and helped his sisters.

"I cut my hand on something," said Renée quietly, staring at it. Albret looked at it too.

"You're not bleeding. You'll be all right," said Abraham, but his attention was still on the soldiers. The children tried to wipe off as much mud as possible, but their clothes were soaked through in some parts.

"Why are they here?" asked Renée.

"I don't want to know," said Abraham.

"Why not?" asked Albret.

"They only bring bad news when they come,"

said Abraham, sighing deeply. "Let's just finish our errand and get home." The city bells rang slowly in the distance, almost moaning for the people to come and hear.

When they finally pulled open the door of the bakery and sniffed all sorts of wonderful bakery smells, everyone cheerfully greeted them and then, noticing the mud, asked the children what had happened. As Abraham explained and the baker filled the buckets with flour, the twins opened the door just a bit and peered out where they could see the soldiers gathered in the public square with people all around them.

"What are they saying?" Renée whispered to Albret.

"I can't hear," she answered.

"Abraham," asked Albret, "may we stand outside, just in front of the shop?"

"Yes. Go ahead, but just in front of the shop," he said.

The girls held hands tightly, stepped outside quickly, and strained to hear what the soldiers were announcing. The one soldier speaking was dressed more colorfully than the others and spoke with an accent from another part of France. The girls stood listening for a long time. Finally, Abraham's voice came from behind them.

"So, what are they announcing?" he asked.

"Listen," said Renée. "You tell us. I don't understand . . . something about . . . soldiers in houses."

Abraham, with a very worried look, started

walking closer to the crowd. Renée and Albret quickly followed, holding onto the buckets now full with flour. For a while they all stood at the edge of the crowd of people listening carefully. The twins were too short to see anything or hear much at all. Sometimes they heard the people around them happily cheering the speaker's words.

Then suddenly, Abraham kneeled down, pulled the sisters together, and said, "We must go quickly. This is very bad. I must tell Father and Mother."

"What did they say?" asked Renée.

"No time to talk now. We must hurry. I'll tell you later."

They ran all the way home, through the narrow streets and mud, holding tightly on to one another and the flour buckets.

"Mamá, Mamá," shouted the girls as they neared the front door of their house.

"Mamá," said Abraham, breathing heavily from the run.

"What is it? What are you so excited about? Why are you covered with mud?" Mother asked quickly.

The twins, with tired legs, plopped down on the floor by the door. Abraham, trying to control his breathing, started, "The King . . . is sending . . . soldiers . . . to . . . live . . . in our . . . houses . . . and . . . we must . . . take . . . care . . . of . . . them."

"Oh, is that all?" said Mother waving it off with her hand. "We have heard such threats before, and even if the King does this, God's people have faced much worse. We fear God, not man."

"Hot, hot, hot," shouted baby Guilliaume, staring at Abraham.

"No hot, hot, hot. Everything is fine," said Mother, stroking baby Guilliaume's head. "Children, start preparing for dinner. Father will be home soon. I've made some special pastries for after dinner."

The children busied themselves with their preparations for the evening meal. Soon, they were all greeted with Father's familiar, "Good evening, family."

That night, Father asked Mary to give thanks for the meal. She stood up, brushing her long, brown hair behind her, and thanked the Lord for their meal, parents, house, and the King. For a short while, everyone was quiet, for the children did not speak at the table unless they were spoken to, but they all wanted to hear more about what the King's soldiers had said. Knowing this, Father turned to Abraham and asked him a question.

"How did your errands for your mother go today, Abraham?"

"Very well, Father . . . The King's soldiers knocked us down in the road while we were going for flour, but we were not hurt."

Renée remembered the cut on her hand.

"Father," said Abraham, "did you see the King's soldiers? Many people were gathered in the public square, and the herald read the King's declaration, and the King is going to station his soldiers in our homes, and . . . "

Not looking up, Father said, "Yes, Abraham, I was there listening. I heard it all."

"Why is the King going to make soldiers live with us?" asked Albret quietly.

Father thought for a moment, rubbing his eyes. "That is a very good question, Albret." He reached for the heavy family Bible, which sat on its own stool beside his chair. He turned the soft pages carefully until he came to a certain passage and began to read.

He read the history of a certain King, who made a statue out of gold and ordered his people to worship it. This King's soldiers and princes and judges and counselors all gathered to honor and worship the golden statue. The King sent out his herald to declare the King's command. The children were listening, wide-eyed. The King's herald declared that, "Whosoever does not bow down and worship the golden statue shall be thrown into the midst of a fiery furnace to die."

Renée sat listening to Father read and thought of the herald she had seen that day. Albret wondered why people would sing to a statue. Guilliaume squirmed in Mother's lap.

Father read of three young men from God's people, who refused to worship the statue, since they knew that the true God forbids such worship. When the King discovered that the three young men would not worship his statue, he threatened them to their faces.

Reading more slowly now, Father stressed the

words of the young men as they answered the King, saying, "The God whom we serve is able to deliver us from the burning fiery furnace, and he will deliver us out of your hand, O King. But if not . . . " continued Father, looking at all the big eyes staring at him, "if not, may you know, O King, that we will not worship the golden image which you have set up."

"Father, were they burned?" asked Renée.

"Listen to what happens," and he read on, describing how the evil King threw God's young men into the furnace and how God preserved them from harm and death.

When Father finished, there was a rush of questions and a long discussion.

"Remember, children, what we've learned before. After Adam's sin, God promised that there would be a long war between the people of the woman and the people of the serpent—between the people of God and the people of the enemy. There are only two kinds of people in the world— friends of God and enemies of God. Some enemies are very kind and decent on the outside, though they oppose God in their hearts. So, too, some people pretend on the outside to be friends of God, but on the inside they do not love God's commandments. Only God knows, and we pray that the Lord will change enemies into friends and that He will clean our hearts and make us faithful for His own glory."

Father continued, "So, what you heard from the herald today was just one part of the long attempt by the enemies of God to fight against the friends of God. And our attitude must be the same as those young men we read of in Daniel. If our French King threatens us with death, we will fear God and not man. And even if God should increase our persecution, we will not bow down to the idols that the French King seeks to force on us."

The children were silent. You could almost hear their minds running.

After the meal, they cleaned up and gathered around the fireplace for what Renée and Albret thought was the best part of the day. For a while the family held hands and sang psalms in front of the fire. The children answered their catechism questions they had practiced with Mother earlier in the day. Sometimes Father would tell them amusing or strange stories about faraway lands and animals. After a while, Mary played her flute softly like a gentle sea breeze, and Mother handed out her special pastries. Soon, the fire died down and it was time for everyone to go to sleep.

Upstairs, Mother, Father, and baby Guilliaume slept in one room, and the others slept in the other room. Renée and Albret shared a bed in the corner. Before they fell asleep, they always talked about what had happened that day. This time they had plenty to discuss, and they whispered, back and forth, ever so quietly, so as not to disturb the others. They whispered about the soldiers and the mud and enemies and friends, and how they had forgotten to go by the fish market. They sometimes asked each other catechism questions, or planned their gardens, or told animal stories of their own. Soon, their eyes grew very heavy and tired, and they fell asleep in the middle of a whisper.

CHAPTER TWO

High Calling

Father quietly crept up the stairs, hesitating on a step that creaked particularly loudly. He held the squirming lamb Bouclé firmly against his chest. The other children were already awake and downstairs completing their morning chores, but Renée and Albret were still asleep in their corner bed. Father slowly slipped into their room and stood Bouclé at the end of their bed. Two little pairs of feet stuck out from under the covers.

Father gently directed Bouclé's cool nose to the unsuspecting toes. Bouclé first sniffed and then softly licked the soles of the girls' feet. Father quickly left the room and little Bouclé to his task. Bouclé licked four toes but got no response. He gently started nibbling, as lambs will do, staring at the sleeping girls' faces as he did. Slowly, they began to move. Albret opened her eyes and stared but said nothing. Renée squirmed and then squealed, "Hey!" When she realized what it was, she giggled sleepily, and both girls pulled Bouclé up into the bed.

"What are you doing here?" said Albret, stroking Bouclé's forehead. The lamb wiggled.

Soon all the family was sitting down together for breakfast, except Mother. The new baby was to be born soon, and sometimes Mother still became ill and had to rest. When this happened, Mary would prepare the morning and evening meals (most people only ate two meals in those years). Father prayed full and encouraging prayers before and after the meal, and then he and Abraham left to work in the family's fabric shop. Mary would run the house that day and watch over Guilliaume and the twins. After the twins helped Mary clean up, they all went upstairs to visit Mother, who greeted them with a tired smile. The twins wanted to help their Mother in some way.

"We could sweep?" asked Albret.

"And change your bed sheets?" added Renée.

All agreed. Mary would work downstairs, cleaning and preparing, and then study her Latin lessons by herself. Albret and Renée would try to help clean upstairs, though Mary would have to put the finishing touches on some of their work.

The broom was really too big for Albret, but she tried ever so hard to sweep the smooth, wooden floor. Sometimes the broom would knock against walls and furniture, but no one could take the broom from her. She was determined. Renée found a dusting cloth and, sometimes standing on a stool, she cleaned the tops of the dresser and other pieces of furniture in the room. Finally, the twins removed the bed sheets from around Mother, bundled them up, and took them down to Mary. They unfolded new sheets and blankets and stood on opposite sides of the bed to stretch them out. Mother was feeling better now, and the three of them talked.

"Mamá, when you were a little girl, did you help your mother clean?" asked Albret. She knew the answer to the question, but she always liked hearing about what her Mother did as a child.

"Oh yes, my mother was an excellent teacher. She kept a beautiful home . . . ," and then she described a time, when she was just older than Mary, that she, her mother, and her sisters had protected their house during a storm that had ripped holes in their old roof.

"Did we ever see your mother?" asked Renée.

"No . . . she died long before you were born. I didn't even see her when she died."

"Why not? You were with Father then?" said Albret.

"No . . . I was away," Mother said quietly, knowing that this answer wouldn't satisfy her girls.

"You were away from your mother and not with Father? What were you doing?" Renée wondered.

Mother was silent for a few moments, lost in her thoughts.

"Mamá?"

"Well, my loves, you see . . . when I was several years older than Mary, my parents sent me away to a . . . a place where many young girls were sent to . . . be kept separated from everything else and serve a church and a god forever."

"It's good to serve God," said Renée.

Mother tried to explain, "But God tells us

how he is to be served and worshipped, and this place, called a convent, was not pleasing to God; it was not faithful to His commandments."

"Why was it not faithful?" asked Albret.

"There once were many convents. Many parents, who were ignorant of Scripture, sent their daughters to these places. Many people used to believe, and some still do believe, that life in a convent is holier than a life of marriage and children. But God in Scripture never commands His people to live in that way. Instead he tells us that we can honor Him by marrying, working hard, loving our children, and serving our neighbors."

The girls asked questions over each other and a "How did you get out?" came through.

"One of my older sisters, your Aunt Martha, who was already married and had left the old unfaithful ways of worshipping God, kept writing to me, trying to explain Scripture more clearly. After several years, I began to listen, read, and understand, and finally when I decided to leave, she arranged with her husband and several good soldiers to help me escape, since the convent would not let me go. And, one cool starless night, we escaped on horseback through the forest. The Lord has been exceedingly merciful to me."

Renée and Albret sat on the bed staring at their mother and thinking. Just then there was a knock at the door.

"We are here. We are here," came two other voices.

"Oh welcome, come see how my girls have

taken care of me." In came Mother's younger sister, Aunt Annet, and their friend Lea, a woman whose job it was to help Mother when it was time to have the baby. Though Aunt Annet was younger than Mother and had four children of her own, her deep, dark eyes and graying, blonde hair made her look older. She had the nicest, biggest smile of anyone the twins knew. Lea was pleasant and spoke very fast, but she was always more serious and worrisome. They had come to check on Mother and the baby inside her.

Mother explained, "We were just discussing the old days—the convent days."

"Ooooh, I see," said Aunt Annet with raised eyebrows.

"Aunt Annet left a convent too," said Mother.

"Did you escape on horseback too?"

"No, I can't say I did. My convent allowed me to leave peacefully . . . I have always been grateful for God's graciousness to me in that. Nowadays, your mother and I are dedicated to much more important and God-pleasing service . . . Madelaine, do you remember that saying from the old German . . . 'There is no power on earth that is nobler or greater than that of parents!'" they said together.

"And," Mother added, "don't forget the teacher Menius: 'The diligent rearing of children is the greatest service to the world, both in spiritual and temporal affairs, both for the present life and for posterity.'"

They both laughed. They surprised themselves

that they had remembered these truths that they had lived but not said for many years. The twins enjoyed this all very much. They chatted for a few more minutes and then Lea asked if Mother was ready to be examined.

"Yes. Renée, Albret, thank you for your help," said Mother. "Now I need some privacy for a few minutes. Would you please excuse us." The girls were used to this. Without a word, they hopped down from the bed and went downstairs.

Mary was busy studying so they decided to go outside and check their gardens. Everything was in order and growing nicely. Renée pulled up a small carrot and started eating it. It was sweet and crunchy. She offered some to Albret, who finished it.

"I know," suggested Albret, "Let's make poppy necklaces for Mother." Renée agreed. Since their poppies were bright orange and yellow, they each would make a necklace of one color. They sat on their knees beside the little walls of poppies and patiently weaved and knotted poppy stems into longer and longer pieces. After what seemed like a long time, they finished their necklaces, tying the ends of each piece together to make a circle. As they made a few final adjustments, Mother came to the back door, but she couldn't see what they were making.

"Girls, come on in, I want you to help me with something." She went back into the cooking area.

The girls didn't come immediately. They just

needed to finish a few more pieces on their necklaces.

"Girls," said Mother, now more sternly, "Slow obedience is disobedience."

"Yes, Mamá. Yes, Mamá." They left their necklaces for the moment and ran inside.

Mother was now feeling much better and her examination had gone well. Aunt Annet and Lea had gone on their way. Mary was stirring something on the iron stove.

"Girls," said Mother, "I want you to help me prepare a meal to take to the Boucher (boo-SHAY) family."

The Boucher family lived several streets away and were part of the same church as the Martineaus. Monsieur Boucher had been very ill for several months and was not able to continue as a fisherman, though Madame Boucher still sold special breads at their family stand. Nevertheless, it became harder for them to care for their children's needs, so, from the beginning, all the other families in the church made sure that the Bouchers were well taken care of. The women regularly helped out with cooked meals, clothing, and medical help, and the men provided chopped wood, fish, and money. Today, Mother and the girls would prepare two evening meals, one for the Boucher family and one for themselves.

When they were ready to take the meal over, Mary went down to the Martineau's wine cellar and pulled out a nice bottle of wine. Since Mother couldn't walk all the way to the Boucher home, Mary and the twins went together. Mary carried the big basket of food, Renée carried the pastries, and Albret carried the wine. As always, the Boucher family was very thankful for the help. Madame Boucher kissed the three girls on their foreheads, and the two Boucher girls walked back halfway with Mary and the twins.

When they got back, the twins ran to finish their Poppy necklaces, and then presented them to Mother who said that they were the most beautiful pieces of jewelry she had ever seen.

After dinner and singing that night, with special prayers for the Boucher family, Mother and Father tucked the children into their beds. As Mother was kissing the twins, she said with a solemn smile,

"Tomorrow is a very special day, my girls."

"Why is tomorrow special?" asked Albret.

"You will see. Now, it's time to sleep."

The twins couldn't sleep at first, trying to guess what was special about tomorrow. It wasn't the Lord's Day. Was the baby coming? Was Uncle Philippe coming to visit? They couldn't tell whether Mother was happy or sad about tomorrow. Oh, well.

For a while, they quietly whispered some of their catechism questions back and forth to one another.

"What is the chief end of human life?" whispered Renée.

"To know God by whom men were created," said Albret.

"What is the highest good of man?" asked Renée.

"The very same thing," said Albret.

"Why do you hold that to be the highest good?" asked Renée.

"Because without it our condition is worse than that of the brutes," said Albret.

"Then we clearly see that nothing worse can happen to a man than not to live to God," said Renée.

"It is so," said Albret.

"What is the true and right knowledge of God?" asked Renée.

"When he is so known that due honor is paid to him," said Albret.

That last catechism answer made them think of their mother. That night they would dream of the convent story.

CHAPTER THREE

The Misunderstanding

Nothing special had yet happened that morning. Renée and Albret sat on the front step of their house trying to figure out why Mother had said that this day would be special. The morning meal was a little strange, they thought, because neither Father, Mother, Abraham, nor Mary ate anything. Everything else was normal. No baby had appeared yet. Soon the twins' thoughts wandered off.

Albret pulled out a small piece of white paper that Abraham had given to the girls. Not many people, especially children, had paper, but several of Abraham's friends were excellent paper makers. Most paper at that time was rather yellow, but the French, especially the Huguenots, were now producing fine, white paper. The girls ran their small hands over it and felt the texture. They held it up to the sunlight and could see its weave.

A few moments later, the girls heard the sound of voices coming down the street—young voices, girls' voices. The twins stood up from the cool step, with Albret ever so carefully tucking the paper back in her pocket, and walked a few steps to the front of their property. Peering down the avenue, they could see a group of girls coming up the road, singing and laughing. Some of the girls were older, some the twins' age, but what was most interesting about the little parade were all the colors. Each girl wore a collection of yellow, blue, red, and orange cloaks and scarves, flowing all about them like dancing flags. The parade of girls was getting larger, and the pretty singing was getting louder.

This must be it, thought Renée. This must be the special thing that Mother mentioned. The girls just stared and smiled as the loose rows of girls holding hands walked by, returning pleasant smiles. Albret recognized some of the girls from Father's shop. Renée had seen many of them at the fish market. Some of them called out the twins' names and waved. The girls started jumping and waving back; they wanted to join in.

Four smiling girls, whom the twins knew by name but didn't know much else about them, broke away from the group and came over to speak to Renée and Albret.

"Hello, Hello," everyone greeted loudly.

One of the four, Maria Gontier, spoke first.

"Are you going to join us? Get Mary and some colors and come along. We're going to the special Feast Day celebration in the town square!"

"Yes, Mamá told us about this," Albret said excitedly.

"What will we do at the festival?" asked Renée.

"There will be singing, dancing, special foods, fun things to do," explained little Catherine Naudé, draped in green scarves.

An older girl, Michelle Caire, described one Feast Day—Fools Day—as a day on which a pretend church service is performed by pretend fools.

"The choirboys dress someone up as a Fools' Bishop and baptize him with buckets of water. Others wear old, torn church clothes inside out and hold their books upside down and read them through silly, orange-peel glasses. Instead of singing hymns, they make up funny words and shout. It is quite fun. I don't know if we will do that today, but I hope so."

This sounded strange but the girls were still excited.

Another girl answered Michelle. "No, they only did those things for the Feast of Fools. Today is St. Bartholomew's Day! We'll have singing and dancing!"

"Quickly, come along. We'll wait," said Maria.

"Okay, wait. I think our Mamá is getting our things! We'll be right back. Don't go without us," said Renée.

The twins ran up the steps and into the house and found Mother upstairs with Mary and Guilliaume.

"Mamá, we found out, we found out! You told us today was special. Are we all going to St. Bartholomew's Feast Day?" asked Albret.

"Doooeee," shouted Guilliaume. He clapped his hands on his head and pointed.

"Do we have fancy colors to wear?" asked Renée.

Mother's face went pale. Mary looked

shocked. Mother covered her mouth with her hand and walked around for a moment, thinking and looking very worried. Then she gently pulled the twins toward her and slowly sat down in her wooden chair next to the dresser.

"My dear girls . . . I know . . . I am sorry that I wasn't clearer when I said that today would be special. I know that you are very excited right now . . . but sometimes things may at first look pleasant, though they are really not."

The girls didn't understand.

Mother tried again, "This Feast Day they are celebrating is not a good day for us. For some people this day is a happy one, but for us and our community, our church, it is a very sad day."

"Why, Mamá?"

"Do you remember the King's soldiers the other day?"

They nodded.

"A long time ago, the King used this day to kill many, many people—men, women, and children—who share our faith. Your father's great grandfather was killed on this day because he followed the Lord and not the old idolatry of the Roman Church. So . . . today is special because we remember what happened on this day so long ago. It is a day of fasting—a day when we don't eat so that we can devote that time to prayer. We will have some friends over tonight, and you will hear more about what happened on St. Bartholomew's Day. But we cannot join with those who rejoice on this day. . . . Do you see?"

she ended with a sad smile.

"This is a holiday for the enemies of God?" asked Albret.

Mother could hear the sweet singing voices outside.

In a low voice, Mother answered, "Yes, my love, it is. Some enemies can be very kind, and we must be kind to them, but for the Lord's sake, we cannot share in their unfaithfulness."

"No, I don't want that," said Albret.

"Me either," agreed Renée.

"The Lord gives us His commands to make us happy," Mother encouraged. The twins left the room and ran downstairs to meet three girls who were still waiting. One had already left.

"Come on," they yelled.

"Sorry, we are not going . . . We . . . This is a sad day for us. Long ago the King killed many Christians on this day. That is not a thing to be happy about," said Renée with humble boldness.

"Our . . . grandfather was a friend of the Lord, but the wicked King killed him," added Albret.

The three girls looked at each other and began to laugh at the twins.

"Oh . . . they're Huguenots," said Catherine with a changed look in her eye. "Well, we're going to sing and dance. You stay here with your silly family."

Maria leaned toward their faces and sang rudely, "Huguenot, Huguenot, not worth a huguenot penny." The three laughed again and ran off toward the town square.

The twins stood there for a moment staring at the ground. Then they each put an arm around the other's shoulder and slowly walked over to their gardens. Why did those girls have to be so rude? After tinkering in their gardens for a moment, they both went back to be near Mother.

Early that evening, family and friends began to arrive at the Martineau home. Uncle Philippe and Aunt Catherine, along with their four daughters came in from their farm. Uncle Gaston, Aunt Annet, and their four children came in quietly, and everyone found seats or floor space on which to sit. A little while later, two elders, Monsieur Pasquier (PAAS-ki-ay) and Monsieur Morin (mo-RAN), from the church and their families also joined the gathering.

As Father welcomed these last guests inside, he caught sight of Monsieur Robiquet (ROBE-i-kay) staring at him from across the street. Monsieur Robiquet was a kind neighbor, but served as a deacon in the local Roman church.

"Your pretended reformed religion," he grumbled, shaking his head at Father, as he headed back inside his home. Father smiled and waved.

Though it was time for the evening meal, Elder Pasquier explained how the Lord had commanded His people to observe days of fasting—no eating—at times in order to remember and devote that time to prayer and worship. None of the adults or older children, including Abraham and Mary, had eaten anything that day, but instead had gladly given the day over to long times of prayer.

They all sang psalms together, holding hands happily. Everyone showed great thankfulness and reverence for the Lord.

Soon Father and Uncle Philippe told the story of the St. Bartholomew's Day Massacre of nearly one hundred years before their time when the blood of God's people flowed in the streets of many cities in France, including their own city, La Rochelle.

The killing started in Paris by the wicked plans of Queen Catherine. During the night, the King's soldiers started killing Huguenot pastors and leaders and throwing their bodies into the city's large river. From the high palace windows, the King and his family excitedly watched the killings in the streets. By the morning of St. Bartholomew's Day itself, large groups of people were helping to stab or shoot Huguenot men, women, and children in and around Paris. The wild groups of killers carried white crosses of the Roman church as they murdered many Christians of "the pretended reformed religion," as the King and Roman church called them.

The fathers especially reminded everyone that they were to love, respect, and pray for the King and those in the Roman church, even though they harmed Christians at times.

"Even more importantly, we will trust the Lord and know His command that we are not to fear those who can kill the body, but we are to fear and respect the Lord alone," said Elder Pasquier.

The evening ended with more prayer, singing, and thanksgiving. Everyone stayed very late, until the wild celebrations in town had died down. The many Feast Days almost always ended in rioting and violence. Since they lived on a farm outside the city, Uncle Philippe, Aunt Catherine, and their children would spend the night with the Martineaus, but the others left to their nearby houses.

The twins sat on Mother's lap, thinking about all that had gone on that night. Father sat beside Mother.

Renée asked, "Could I be a queen someday?"

"With the Lord, all things are possible," smiled Father.

"We could be good queens together," added Albret.

"And our soldiers would protect you and Father and all the Christians," said Renée.

"You remember that you were named after very good Christian rulers," reminded Mother.

They both remembered that well.

"But, my poppies," Mother began, "queens, kings, princes, soldiers, and governments come and go like the wind. They are here one moment and gone the next. The work of good queens is often quickly forgotten, but a parent's prayers and teaching can influence a thousand generations."

The girls liked that.

CHAPTER FOUR

Rahab's Sisters

Several weeks had passed, and the summer waned, though it was still warm. One night, the twins awoke to loud voices in the house. They both sat up and tried to listen.

"You will have to go for Lea, the midwife," Father ordered Abraham. "I will stay by Mother's side."

"What of the curfew and the King's soldiers?" asked Abraham.

"Stay low and hide in the shadows," said Father.

"Yes, I can do that well," agreed Abraham with determination. He ran back into the children's bedroom, grabbed his wrap and hat, and hurried downstairs. He shut the front door behind him, looked to the street, and immediately froze still on the doorstep. At that same moment, a dragoon—one of the King's soldiers—was slowly passing by on his horse.

"And where did you think you were going?" asked the dragoon coldly.

Abraham grew angry but said nothing at first. "I need to get a midwife for my mother," he tried.

"Ahhh . . . ," the soldier paused, rubbing his horse's neck, "you should have thought of that before now . . . Yes? Back inside little man. Not every mother needs a midwife."

Abraham turned and went back inside. It was useless to argue with a dragoon. Father was even angrier when he heard. Abraham and Father tried to figure out what to do next. They couldn't send Father, since he would be instantly jailed for a long time. They couldn't send Mary, since the dragoons were known to harm young ladies. The twins were just too young.

"We're not too young, Father," said Albret. "We could hide better than Abraham, since we're smaller."

"We would hold hands all the way, and be able to help each other," said Renée.

Father refused to even consider it, but Mother was moaning louder now. It appeared that something was wrong with this baby, since Mother was much better when the other children were born. Father was angry with himself for not planning better, and now his dear wife was suffering for it. He slammed his fist down on the kitchen table; one cup tipped onto the floor and smashed. He didn't even notice. The children all sat quietly waiting, while Father thought.

"Renée! Albret! You will have to go. We have no other choices. The dragoons will not hurt you. Do you remember where Lea lives?"

Albret did. Renée didn't.

"You will go out the back door, through the rear plots, to the streets. Stay near the shop walls on the streets. Lea will know the best way back. Listen to her."

"Yes, Father, we can do it," said Albret.

"We want to help Mamá," said Renée.

Dressed alike, wearing white bonnets, they took their brown wraps, though it was really too warm to wear them. They slipped out the back door holding hands excitedly. They ran through several neighbors' rear plots, stepping carefully around gardens, and came to the first street they had to cross. They slowly peered around the corner to check for dragoons, and when none was to be seen, they ran, still holding hands, down the street and across another.

They moved like two careful cats down a street of shops, sometimes stopping at the slightest sound. They had to keep moving, past the baker, past the fabric shop, and through the empty fish market. Then they heard it—the sound of a soldier and horse. Renée looked one way, Albret the other. Quickly the twins slipped into the darkness of the nearest shop doorway. Clop-clop, clop-clop—the soldier was going to pass right by the doorway in which they were hiding. The twins pressed themselves deeper into the darkness, covering their white bonnets with their dark wraps. He came closer and closer, and, in a moment, was passing right in front of the doorway. The girls held their breath and prayed silently. Then the horse sounds grew quieter and quieter, as the soldier moved down the street. When he was far enough away, they started running down the street again, thinking of their mother.

Finally, they passed by several other streets

and arrived at the last crossing, almost at Lea's house. Renée stopped running to look carefully around this corner, but Albret darted into the street without stopping.

Another dragoon's horse whinnied and stopped short. The soldier had to move the horse's head out of the way to even see the small girl in his path. Albret stood frozen. Renée remained hidden around the corner behind a thick ivy plant.

The dragoon was startled, and, so, angrily he demanded, "You there . . . where are . . . you are not to be out here!"

Albret stood still, not so much afraid, as thinking what to do.

"I think I should throw you in the jail," he lied.

"My mother needs help. I must go," said Albret.

"My mother needs help too," said the dragoon, "but not during a curfew." He slid off his horse and noticed his captain on horseback at the end of the street. The dragoon firmly grabbed Albret's arm and pulled her beside his horse.

"Don't even think about running away," he threatened. He grabbed a free leather strap hanging from his saddle and wrapped it around her arm, tying a large knot, to keep her from leaving.

"I'll be right back to take you home," he said and headed over to his captain.

When he was far enough away, Albret looked over to Renée. "Go on," she whispered. "Go get Lea."

"You know the way. I don't," scolded Renée.

Albret was upset but not crying. She looked back to her sister just as Renée had an idea.

Round-eyed, Renée whispered, "Let's switch places," describing the switch with her hands. Albret smiled, realizing the plan.

"Can you get the strap off?" Renée asked quietly. Albret nodded and started squirming out of it, though it hurt. If both girls ran off, the dragoons would start a search up every street, and the sisters would never be able to reach Lea. If the twins merely switched places, the soldier would not become suspicious and just take the one back to the house. But, if they were caught switching, however, both would be returned home. The dragoon had reached his captain, and the two soldiers stood chuckling over the little "criminal" in their custody.

Albret was now loose, though she held the strap to make it look like she was still tied. She glanced over at Renée. Renée was ready. They looked at the dragoons up the street and waited for them to turn away. Renée was only five big steps away, behind the wall. They watched the soldiers. Finally, one of the dragoons laughed hard and bent over, and the other looked the other way. Renée moved swiftly, Albret handed her the strap and slid behind the wall. The horse next to them whinnied loudly. Renée looked up to see the dragoons staring at the horse from up the street. Did they see the switch? Should she just run? She still needed to slide her arm in the knot, but he was staring and started walking back to-

ward her. Renée slowly turned her body so that
her wrap and body covered her arm, and in went
her arm snugly.

"Stop," ordered the dragoon. "Stop moving
around. You'll frighten my horse."

The switch had worked. Albret had already
run down the other street. She would have to
circle back out of view, being wary of other dragoons.

"Tell me where you live," the dragoon demanded. "I don't have time to waste on this nonsense."

"I think it's up that way," she pointed.

"Come along." He hoisted her onto the horse.

Albret knocked on Lea's back door while
opening it and ran upstairs. Lea was used to this,
and she was almost instantly ready to go. Lea also
knew many ways to avoid the dragoons. At that
time, the King had forbidden any Huguenot, like
Lea, to work as a midwife. Instead, by permit-
ting only midwives from the Roman Church, the
King sought to make sure that any new children
would be baptized into the Roman Church. But
Father would not stand for that.

Lea and Albret moved so quickly that they
arrived before Renée. That was part of Renée's
plan. She knew that she had to at least keep her
dragoon busy so that he might not have the chance
to bother Albret and Lea, so she directed him to
the Martineau house the long way.

When Renée finally arrived, the dragoon let
her down and threatened again to put her in prison

next time. Abraham opened the door, with Albret peering around his side toward her twin and the dragoon. Renée was quickly inside. For a moment, the dragoon wasn't exactly sure what he saw in the doorway. He rubbed his eyes. *It's late. I must be tired*, he thought and rode away.

Lea was a great help for Mother, though there still were problems with the baby. Father sat next to Mother, holding her hand. The four children had gathered in their room to pray for Mother. Guilliaume was asleep in the corner. Abraham started by thanking the Lord for such a wonderful Mother and pleaded for her and the baby. Mary followed by praying a psalm of help. Albret and Renée thanked the Lord for their safety and for Lea's help. They were all so tired.

A while later, Renée and Albret woke from a short sleep. It was now getting lighter outside. Abraham and Mary hadn't moved from their places or fallen asleep. Mary told the twins that the baby wasn't born yet and that everyone was still concerned for Mother and the baby.

A few moments later everyone breathed easier, and the whole room seemed brighter. They heard the new baby crying. That was good. The baby sounded healthy, Mary explained to the twins. They still waited patiently in their room for what seemed like a very long time. Finally, Abraham suggested that they keep praying for Mother and the baby.

In the middle of the prayer, Father opened their door and, smiling broadly, called them to see Mother and the new baby sister Phoebe (FEE-bee). Mother and baby were fine.

After the sun rose and everything had settled down, Lea, the midwife, always chattering quickly like a baby bird, held her bottle of olive oil used for the baby's eyes and was about to leave. She reminded Mother, "Remember to smear Phoebe's body with nut oil. That will harden her skin so that she won't be easily cut or bruised. And in three or four days when her umbilical cord falls off, make a paste of wood ashes, mussels, and burned calf's hoof to treat the navel."

Mother listened politely, but she wasn't new to having babies. All the children took turns holding the new baby, except for Guilliaume. He tried once with Father's help, but quickly gave the baby back, shaking his head, "Hot, hot, hot."

CHAPTER FIVE

Stars and Sand

A few days later the twins spent most of the day at the family's fabric shop with Father, while Mother rested with the new baby. Before leaving for the shop that morning, though, they needed to harvest some of the vegetables from their gardens. The morning sun was slowly shining through the cool fog that draped itself all around the townhomes. The girls each pulled and piled carrots, onions, and turnips, brushing off the dirt from each. They snapped plenty of pea pods into one middle pile, snacking on cool, sweet peas as they worked. Though they had attempted to grow several grapevines with the help of Uncle Philippe, these hadn't turned out very well this season. Maybe next year.

Though the sun had only been up a short while, Guilliaume came outside with the girls and played quietly with sticks and dirt near the edge of the back plot. When the sisters had taken up all the ripe vegetables, leaving others for later weeks, they gathered them in their aprons and headed for the cooking area. Later they would help Mother and Mary clean, store, and cook their harvest. They were pleased with the work of their hands.

"I didn't see Bouclé this morning," said Albret.

"Maybe he is in front," said Renée, not worried.

They looked in the front and back but couldn't find him. Apparently, he had chewed through the rope that held him. Now they were worried. They stayed close to their house and tried to find him in other yards, but he was nowhere to be found. Mother gave them permission to look up the street and around the corner. They asked neighbors, but no one had seen him. In the end, they came back in the house weeping, because they couldn't find Bouclé and thought they would never see their soft, little friend again. Did he run away? Did someone take him? No one knew. Abraham and Father took up the search again, up and down the plots, but they couldn't find him either.

Everyone tried to comfort the sad twins, except for Guilliaume. He was still playing with his dirt and sticks, quite unaware of the entire fuss. No one had thought to ask Guilliaume. Finally, he came in the house, brushing off the mud caked on his robe.

"Out! Out! Do that outside Guilliaume!" said Mother, as she pushed him by his shoulders. As he was being moved out, he noticed over his shoulder that the girls were crying. He thought they had been spanked. When he came back in, he went over to them and looked up under their hands that covered their faces and patted their backs to console them.

"Bouclé is gone, GeeGee," wept Albret.

Guilliaume looked confused.

"Bouclé ran away, and we can't find him," explained Renée, wiping her nose.

He still looked confused, which was common for Guilliaume.

"Daaa," said Guilliaume, pointing outside.

Nobody paid any attention to him. He moved toward the back door as if he were going outside.

"No, don't go out now. It's time to eat," said Mother.

"Bookee daaa," said Guilliaume loudly.

"What?" asked Mother. The others now looked at him too.

"Bookee daaa!" insisted Guilliaume again, pointing outside with his chubby finger.

Mary looked out the back window, in the direction where Guilliaume was pointing. And there, well hidden under a low ivy plant along the back of the plot where Guilliaume had been playing, she could just make out the shape of a small lamb.

"He was with Guilliaume!" said Mary. "There's Bouclé at the back, under the ivy."

The twins ran outside and gently pulled the sleeping lamb from the ivy. This didn't at all please the lamb who was quite comfortable and warm where he was. The girls' tears turned into grateful smiles and hugs. Guilliaume still didn't know what the fuss was all about. He just frowned and walked away.

After the morning meal, Father, the twins,

and Abraham headed off for the fabric shop. Along the way, the girls showed Father the dark doorway they had hid in and the place in the street where the dragoon stopped them.

The twins loved the fabric shop with all its intricate weaving machines and had often been there with Mother as she tended to customers. The back of the shop was full of weaving machines, spinners, rollers, yarns, dyes, and many kinds of threads. The front of the store was reserved for showing fabrics and serving customers. On the front counter stood two fat jars of Greek olives, which Father sold for a very low price to help bring people into the store.

Father and three apprentices—one of which was Abraham—worked in the back creating very fine fabrics. The King had forbidden Huguenots to work as doctors, lawyers, city officials, pharmacists, and many other positions, so, instead, they turned their skills to other trades, such as fabric and paper production.

Everyone in the shop, from Father to the newest apprentice, worked very hard, and everyone's muscles were always sore by the end of the day. That's how Father determined a good day's work—if you weren't tired, then it wasn't really work. But no one worked just for himself or simply for money. They understood, almost without thinking, that they labored and created beautiful materials for the glory of God.

The twins stayed at the shop all afternoon doing small chores, playing with leftover fabric pieces, and eating olives. They pieced the leftover fabric into pretend outfits and animal skins.

Many people visited the store that day, and almost everyone asked the girls about their new baby sister, Phoebe. The girls sparkled as they described the baby's blue eyes and thick, black hair.

"Will we see Phoebe at church this Lord's Day?" asked a friend, while Father wrapped her fabric.

"Oh yes, she'll be there. We plan to have the elders baptize her this Sunday, Lord willing. We'll show her off then," said Father. He always carefully helped each customer and made sure that they were very pleased with their purchases. Everyone, Christians and non-Christians, respected Father as a man of strength and honesty. He, in turn, was kind and respectful to every customer, but he was not slavish or flattering. His face and eyes seemed to naturally show his honesty, wisdom, and self-discipline. Upon first meeting him, some people were a little afraid, but as soon as he showed one of his wide, weathered smiles, people felt right at home.

Father left Abraham to close the shop that night, and he and the girls left a little early, but they didn't take the normal way home. The late afternoon sun had set, the stars were coming out, and a warm summer wind blew from the ocean.

"Why aren't we going the usual way?" said Renée.

"It's such a beautiful summer evening," said

Father, "that I wanted to walk by the harbor beach."

The girls each held one of Father's hands, and they walked for quite a while. Little legs started to get tired. Finally they came to a sandy beach on the south harbor side of La Rochelle. They sat down and rested, staring at the two towers, St. Nicholas and Chain Tower, standing stoutly at the mouth of the harbor. At night, the harbor-keepers would raise a giant chain between the towers so as to protect the harbor at night. Several tall ships swayed gently in the harbor, and the breeze seemed even warmer now, though it was dark. An unbelievable amount of stars was emerging.

"Girls, I brought you out here so you could really see these stars," said Father. "Have you ever seen such a sight? You are usually indoors at this time."

Renée and Albret stared at them.

"They are like little jewels," said Renée.

"Many, many diamonds," said Albret. They all sat there for a moment quietly.

"Can you feel the sand in your hands?" Father asked in a calm, serious voice.

They nodded and slowly let some sand trickle through their fingers.

"It's warm," said Renée. Another breeze filled them with the rich smell of the ocean.

"Girls, it's very important that you remember these stars and this sand," Father said solemnly.

The girls looked at him waiting for an explanation. His eyes were moist.

Very slowly, he started, "The other night on St. Bartholomew's Day we spoke of many sad things . . . and soon you may see more . . . We don't know what the future holds, but whatever happens I will need you to be strong and faithful to the Lord . . . There may be many tears. We don't know what the King may do. But whatever happens, I want you to remember this sand and these stars." He sighed deeply.

"Do you remember Abraham in the Scriptures? The Lord promised Abraham that someday the friends of God would be as numerous as the stars in the sky and the sand on the beach. Someday there'll be so many friends that there will be very few, if any, wicked kings, hypocrites, and enemies . . . Some day the Lord will wipe away all of our tears, because He will keep His promise to Abraham . . . So, wherever we are, remember this place. Will you promise me that?" Father asked, staring at the stars.

"Yes," the twins said thoughtfully. They sat in silence, thinking for a while. They watched a shooting star over by the horizon.

"There's something else about the sand and stars. The Lord also promised that He would show His mercy and blessings to Abraham's children— all those who trust God the way Abraham did, along with their children. The Lord told us to place His mark on all Abraham's children so we can separate the friends from the enemies and remember that it is the Lord who cleans our hearts, saves us, and not we ourselves. That's why we baptized you, when you were born. God places His mark on His people, keeping His holy promises to Abraham of so long ago."

"And Phoebe?" asked Albret.

"That's right. On this Lord's Day we will take Phoebe to church and see to it that she too will be baptized and counted as a child of Abraham, like one star or one grain of sand," he said with a smile. "And the Lord promised that He will be merciful to the children of Abraham for a thousand generations—many, many, many births. So, I pray that He would do that in our family for a thousand generations. And will you pray for your children and their children and teach them to be faithful to the Lord?"

"Yes," they said.

"And I'll tell them to tell their children to pray," added Albret.

The three of them sat quietly for a moment. A light breeze warmed their faces.

With hope and sadness in his voice, Father said, "So, always remember those stars and this sand." He hugged both girls at the same time with a big bear hug.

"Now, let's go home and see that new girl of ours again."

CHAPTER SIX

Church Rest

The Lord's Day was always the best day of the week. The Martineaus would be together for the whole day, rejoicing, singing, and learning. They would meet with other close friends at church to thank and honor the Lord for all that He had done during the past week, and all that He would do in the future.

As the twins readied themselves with crisp bonnets and fresh dresses, the sun shone brightly in a clear sky, though Father noted that rain clouds were churning on the horizon.

At the door, Father waved at Monsieur Robiquet, who was standing across the street, but the Roman deacon pretended not to see. When everyone was ready, all the Martineaus started down the street together. Abraham and Mary walked in front, Mother and Father followed behind them holding Phoebe and Guilliaume, and the twins tagged alongside them all, holding hands.

"What will the Pastor preach about today?" asked Albret.

"I heard that he will preach on glorifying God," said Father.

The girls thought about that. The family passed other families going to the Roman Church in the other direction, and everyone greeted each other kindly. At this time, all the thousands of Huguenots in La Rochelle had to meet in churches held in homes. A year prior, the King had forcibly closed the large, Huguenot church building in the city. By closing that building, the officials had assumed that the Huguenots would return to the Roman Church. Some did, but thousands of others didn't. Throughout France, the King gave local officials the authority to shut down any Huguenot church whose pastor preached anything slightly contrary to the King, and the officials were sure to have someone from the Roman Church sit in and listen to every Huguenot service.

When the Martineaus turned a corner, there stood the house where they worshipped, not large and not covered with statues or pictures. It showed warmth from within. After greeting long-time friends, the Martineaus took their family seats on the second bench from the back. They filled the entire bench.

The worship service opened with a short prayer by Elder Pasquier. Far from the hustle and bustle of daily life, and far from childish pictures, candles, and statues, the congregation worshipped in simple beauty. Words—in all their power and elegance—surrounded and completely filled each person. Words—in song, prayer, exhortation, and preaching—richly drew the congregation into sweet union and communion with their God.

Renée and Albret especially loved to thank God through song. When all the men and women joined as one voice, the twins thought it sounded like a glorious chorus of angels.

After the opening prayer, the congregation took their Geneva Psalters and continued to worship by singing:

> Thou art the King of mercy and grace,
> Reigning omnipotent in every place:
> So come, O King, and our whole being sway;
> Shine on us with the light of thy pure day.

> Thou art the Life, by which alone we live,
> And all our substance and our strength receive,
> O comfort us in death's approaching hour,
> Strong-hearted then to face it by thy pow'r.

> Our hope is in no other save for thee;
> Our faith is built upon thy promise free;
> O grant to us such stronger hope and sure
> That we can boldly conquer and endure.

Generations of faithful Huguenots had sung those words in the face of danger and death.

After several psalms and Scripture readings, Pastor De Laune (duh-LAWN) came forward, along with the other elders, and called Monsieur and Madame Martineau to come forward with baby Phoebe. Pastor De Laune, with his gray hair and brown beard, warmly welcomed the Martineaus, whom he had known for many years. Both Mother and Father smiled widely as the Pastor explained the biblical teaching on baptism. Renée and Albret listened carefully.

"Now our gracious God, not contenting Himself with having adopted us for His children, and received us into his Church, has been pleased to extend his goodness still farther to us, by promising to be our God and the God of our children for a thousand generations."

Albret and Renée looked at each other quickly, remembering the sand and the stars.

" . . . though the children of believers are of the corrupt race of Adam, He nevertheless accepts them in virtue of this covenant, and adopts them into His family. For this reason, the Lord was pleased, since Abraham's time, that in His Church children should receive His mark, the sign of the covenant, which we now represent by baptism . . . "

Guilliaume wiggled to see better from Mary's lap. She told him to sit still.

Pastor De Laune continued, " . . . since the Lord Jesus Christ came down to earth to extend the covenant of salvation over all the world, there is no doubt that our children are heirs of the life which He has promised to us. . . ."

When he finished explaining, as he did so clearly with every baptism, Pastor De Laune asked the congregation to pray with him for the new baby. When he finished, he turned back to Father and Mother and asked, "Do you offer this infant for baptism?"

"We do indeed," they answered.

"Do you promise to be careful to instruct this child in all God's holy doctrine, and generally in all that is contained in the Holy Scriptures of the Old and New Testaments?"

"We do."

"Do you promise to exhort this child to live according to the rule which God has laid down in his law, which is summarily contained in two points—to love God with all our heart and mind and strength, and our neighbor as ourselves, in order that she may dedicate and consecrate herself to glorify the name of God and Jesus Christ and edify her neighbor?"

"We do," said Mother and Father, looking into the Pastor's eyes. Mary felt goose bumps on her arms.

"What name have you given to this child?" asked the Pastor.

"Phoebe Martineau," answered Father.

"Phoebe Martineau, child of the covenant, I baptize thee in the name of the Father, and of the Son, and of the Holy Spirit." As he said this, he gently scooped a handful of water from a bronze cup, and poured it over Phoebe's forehead. Her eyes widened, and she looked around, but she didn't cry. Renée and Albret hugged each other in their excitement. They would have squealed, if they weren't in church.

After the elders and Mother and Father returned to their benches, Elder Pasquier led the congregation in several more psalms, which, after witnessing the glories of a baptism, sounded more angelic than ever.

Soon Pastor De Laune returned to the pulpit and began to teach the people concerning the glory of God. Renée and Albret couldn't always understand his words, but they always listened closely. Sometimes, when they brought their writing slates, they would draw pictures from some of the words Pastor De Laune spoke. When he spoke of a lamb, they would take turns drawing lambs; when he spoke of a lion, they would take turns drawing lions. On the way home, Father would ask them questions about the sermon, so that they could better understand.

As the sermon went on, the rays of sunshine, beaming through the side windows, almost unnoticeably changed their direction after a while. Renée noticed that Pastor De Laune looked very worn and tired. More than usual. Albret softly ran her hand over the smooth, church bench, staring at Pastor De Laune, as he closed, saying, "and in all, to glorify God is chiefly to do these two things: holding Him in all esteem and reverence in our hearts, and serving Him in all outward expressions of honor and duty in our conversation, behavior, and lives.

"To have such high thoughts of His power and greatness as to make us dread and stand in awe of Him, to understand His justice as to make us fear offending Him, to esteem His wisdom as to cause us to bow before His counsel, to embrace such a sense of His mercy and goodness as

to influence our every thought and deed with
regard to Him and our neighbor . . . that is to
glorify God and honor His name . . . Amen.

"Now, as this duty cannot be anywhere performed with such advantage as where the faithful are assembled together for that purpose, let
us close in song . . . "

By the end of the psalm, the sun rays pierc-
ing the room had faded. The rain clouds had started
coming in sooner than expected. After the service, each Martineau went to speak to one or more
friends and gathered around Mother when most
of the people had headed for home. But Father
and Uncle Philippe were still standing with the
Pastor and elders discussing something very serious. Renée noticed no smiles. Albret didn't like
the looks on their faces. Too solemn.

When Father joined the rest of the family,
Mother looked at him with curious eyes.

"More trouble," he said, "This morning some
dragoons have moved into several homes of mem-
bers who are part of one of our sister churches
across town."

He and Mother talked about it all the way
home. As they all neared the house, the rain started
falling fast and heavy. Mother covered baby
Phoebe in her wrap, and they all quickened their
pace through the slippery street. The air turned
cool.

When they arrived home, Abraham started a
big fire that quickly removed the chill from the

house. That afternoon, they ate well and rested. Father made up more funny, animal stories and asked catechism questions of each of the children. Mother had Mary play her flute, and no one wanted her to stop. But something terrible did make her stop.

Late in the afternoon, the Martineaus were startled to hear the most frightful pounding on their front and back doors. Soon the doors burst open, and the whole downstairs was flooded with wet and dirty dragoons. Before Father or Abraham realized what was happening or could rise from their seats, several dragoons had pulled them both across the room and pushed them hard against the side wall. Others backed Mother and the other children up against the rear wall.

"My, aren't you a pretty little Huguenot," said the captain, fingering Mary's hair. Mary stared at the floor, and Mother moved in front of her, angrily pushing the dragoon's arm away. Father started to shout something, but he was slapped silent and held against the wall.

Very slowly, the captain grimaced and spoke, "We are here in the service of King Louis XIV, who has determined to see the conversion of all Huguenot heretics, such as yourselves, in his realm."

He stared at Mother.

"All of La Rochelle will return to the Roman Church and the King, and to proceed with our work of conversion, the King has decreed that we shall shelter under the roofs of his Huguenot subjects."

The captain walked closer to Mother. He gently touched her cheek with his hand. Mother went taut.

"You, Madame, will take good care of us."

Instantly, Father and Abraham broke free from their captors and rushed at the captain as he touched Mother's face. Father and Abraham clawed for the captain, but they never came close. The whole room seemed to move against them at once. Ten dragoons grabbed Abraham and threw him over the table, knocking it over. Ten others flipped Father backwards and laid him flat on the stone floor. Like a flash of silver lightning, every sword was pointed at their necks, ready to run them through.

The captain turned calmly as if nothing had happened. He had the look of death on his face. He raised his finger to give the signal to kill them both, when the front door blew open, and there stood Monsieur Robiquet. The Roman deacon's deep, loud voice filled the room, making them all catch their breath. Guilliaume and Phoebe were now screaming. Renée and Albret cowered, terrified, in the corner.

"Do not mooove!!!" he bellowed. Even the captain froze in his place. He stared directly at the captain, and spoke menacingly. "You, captain, have violated your authority under the King's command. These heretics are officially under my direct supervision as granted by the local authorities."

Monsieur Robiquet was a very big man, and he towered over most of the soldiers. As he moved through the crowd of soldiers, moving them out of his way with his broad shoulders, he approached the captain.

"And who are you?" asked the captain, with a little fear in his voice. Monsieur Robiquet helped Father and Abraham to their feet.

"You know very well what I do, but you are more than welcome to check my credentials with the city authority at your leisure, if you have nothing more important to do. Right now, you are to vacate this home on pain of being stripped of your command!"

The captain hesitated, not knowing what to say. "You don't have the authority to do this!"

Monsieur Robiquet's face became red with anger, but he spoke in a whisper, "You are on very dangerous ground, Monsieur. I could have the King grant me your head, if I wanted it! . . . Need I add that some of your men have given me and others a full account of your drunken slander against the King the other night."

The captain didn't know whether to believe him or not. He couldn't remember what he had said. He decided that this pitiful Huguenot family was not worth the risk.

"Out!" ordered the captain. "But take supplies! We are guaranteed supplies, are we not?" he reminded Monsieur Robiquet. Robiquet nodded in disgust. The dragoons took everything they could get their hands on, food, tools, small furniture, books, even Mary's flute. They would sell all these things for their own profits. The soldiers quickly filed out of the front and back doors, with the captain in the lead. They mounted their horses and rode off quickly. Monsieur Robiquet remained standing in the middle of the room. Everyone else ran over to Father and Abraham.

"You could have killed yourselves," scolded Mother.

"I am fine," said Father, as he gently worked his way through the hugs to Monsieur Robiquet.

"I am forever indebted to you, Monsieur Robiquet," confessed Father, grabbing hold of Robiquet's hand with both of his.

"Mmmm," said Robiquet in a low voice.

"How did you know? I didn't know your position gave you—" said Father.

"Monsieur Martineau," interrupted Robiquet, "I am no friend of yours. I despise your pretended reformed religion as a slap in the face of the Mother Church, but I also despise the work of the dragoons. You and I might someday settle these issues as gentlemen and not barbarians . . . As regards my claims to the captain . . . a trick against fools. Knowing this man's practices, I took a chance that he had been drunk recently and merely spoke in an authoritative voice, though I have no such authority. These men are cowards inside."

"Once again," said Father, "I offer you my greatest thanks as my gentleman neighbor and a man of wisdom and valor . . . I hope we may be genuine friends some day."

"Mmmm," agreed Robiquet, "God has spared your lives this night, but tomorrow they will discover my trick and return. You must leave before first light." Monsieur Robiquet tipped his head respectfully toward Mother, shook Father's hand, turned, and left through the open front door.

Abraham, though severely bruised, walked unsteadily over to the front door and closed it. They all stood in the center of the room and held on tightly to each other. They just stood in complete silence for a while, except for Phoebe's crying.

After several minutes, Father spoke the words of the apostle Paul with great thankfulness. "For our light affliction, which is but for a moment, is working for us a far more exceeding and eternal weight of glory, while we look not at things which are seen, but at the things which are not seen; for the things which are seen are temporal, but the things which are not seen are eternal."

CHAPTER SEVEN

Refuge From the Storm

The stars were still shining faintly as the sky grew brighter. Everyone in the house gathered all the things each could safely carry. Abraham kept listening for the dragoons to return, but the family need not have worried. Though few in the town knew, all the soldiers regularly slept soundly at this time of morning.

"Now remember children," said Mother calmly, "we only need the things we use every day. Lord willing, we will return from Uncle Philippe's farm in a month or soon after the dragoons move on."

Albret and Renée stepped out the back door to shake some bread crumbs out of a light blue tablecloth. Their chattering went silent. Time was short that morning as everyone hurried about, and when the girls didn't return quickly, Mother grew impatient.

"Girls, come back inside. We have work to do," said Mother as she stepped out back, glancing around. There they sat, trying to hold back their tears and be big girls. But tears trickled down their dresses into the trampled flowers and vegetables that had once been their gardens. Carrots and onions and turnips had been kicked out of the ground and mashed into pieces. Last night when the dragoons came, they and their horses had plowed their big, uncaring boots and hoofs in and out, over and over, all through the girls' work. The horses had chewed up the vegetables that they hadn't crushed.

Renée and Albret stared at their once healthy poppies whose petals lay twisted and pressed into the earth. But the sisters didn't make a sound. They just sat in silence, missing the work of their hands. Their gardens had taken so long and seemed to require so much work and love.

They didn't notice Mother. She came behind them and gently pulled them up by their arms. She turned them around and held their little chins in her warm hands, staring into their eyes.

Holding back her own tears for her children, she whispered, "The Lord gives and the Lord takes away, blessed be the name of the Lord."

Looking down, they nodded.

"Lord willing, we will start a new garden next year," said Mother. They would have to wait for next year because this was now harvest time and the fall season was soon upon them. Mother moved them back inside. Time was running out.

Father had quickly run over to Pastor De Laune's home as sunshine appeared over the horizon. Pastor De Laune had already been out helping another family that had been forced to give shelter to a band of dragoons the previous night, and he had been on his way to the Martineau's house, having heard their news. Father met him in the street and told him they were planning to move out to Uncle Philippe's farm for a while, until the dragoons moved on. Pastor De Laune agreed and said that several other families were moving out of town for a while as well.

When Father returned to the house, two elders from the church were there helping to get the family's things in order. They offered to carry bags out to the farm, but Father and Abraham said they would be able to carry the bags without trouble. The son of one of the elders started out to Uncle Philippe's farm to tell him of the Martineau's trouble.

As the Martineaus started down the muddy road, Monsieur Robiquet watched them from his window, thinking that they should have left earlier. Father nodded another thank you to him, and they were off. More clouds were starting to gather overhead, and the fog still divided the sunlight.

To avoid attracting more attention, Father decided that the family should separate into smaller groups and meet again outside the city walls. Renée and Albret each carried a blanket, and they took turns holding the rope attached to Bouclé. Mary carried Phoebe, and Mother carried Guilliaume, sometimes letting him walk a ways. Father and Abraham each carried two large sacks of the family belongings.

Soon they all met outside the town and started following the long, winding, muddy roads to Uncle Philippe's farm. They passed by rain-swelled creeks and a few, smaller vineyards glistening in the remaining sunshine.

After about an hour of walking through the sucking mud, they stopped. No dragoons had followed them or had even known of their leaving town. They sat on an old, broken, stone wall a short way from the road and rested. Mother fed Phoebe and Guilliaume explored the wall, smacking it here and there. Bouclé was tired too, but no one would carry him. Everyone's shoes, stockings, and feet were soaked through with mud, as were the hems of the twins' dresses.

After Phoebe was ready to go, Father and Abraham stood up with their bags again and started slogging along the road. Abraham was sure that the farm couldn't be much farther now.

The rain clouds had continued to gather all morning, and after walking a few more hills, the rain started to fall. It started lightly at first, and then grew harder and harder. They all moved off the road quite a way and found some cover from the rain under a huge, old tree. The pounding rain didn't stop for a long time.

As they waited, they could hear the sounds of a horse and wagon nearing them. Thinking that it might be more dragoons, they pressed themselves out of sight around the tree. Father and Abraham watched carefully. The rain muffled the sound. Abraham watched the road, as the water dripped off the brim of his hat in front of his eyes, but then he turned and glanced up the road in the direction they were heading. There it was!

Uncle Philippe and the elder's son were racing down the muddy road toward town. But the Martineaus could not be seen or heard from where they were hiding, so Abraham dropped his bags, called out, and started running toward the road, waving his hands. The steady rain muffled his cries. Uncle Philippe rushed on by with his wagon. Abraham, now at the road, kept running after him and shouting.

Barely hearing something, the elder's son riding with Uncle Philippe glanced behind him and saw a soaked Abraham waving his arms, getting farther and farther behind the wagon. Father was behind Abraham now as well.

Soon the horse and wagon had turned around and pulled up the road to the waiting Martineaus.

"That was a close one," laughed Uncle Philippe. He slapped his knees with his wide, strong, farm hands, and his whole, wide, red face and bald head seemed to smile. "As soon as I heard the news, I started out for you." Mother hugged him, and he and Father helped everyone get into the back of the wagon. They covered themselves with blankets. The elder's son bid them all farewell, and started off, running back to his home in town. Everyone thanked him heartily.

The ride in the wagon seemed longer than usual, and the rain never let up. But finally, Uncle Philippe, with Father sitting next to him, directed the horse off the main road down another, smaller path. Albret and Renée were now sitting up, uncovered, and could see the farmhouse's warm candle lights sparkling through some trees.

"We're here," they said slowly. And all the others pulled off their blankets and looked around. Uncle Philippe pulled into the stable, and Aunt Catherine and her four daughters came running out to meet them. Hugs and kisses were everywhere.

"You are all so soaked," said Aunt Catherine, "Hurry, hurry, inside. We have dry clothes and a big, warm fire for you."

Three of Uncle Philippe's and Aunt Catherine's daughters—Marthe, Sarah, and Jeanette—were close in age to Albret and Renée. The oldest cousin, Elizabeth, was a little younger than Mary. All four cousins had bright, rosy cheeks and sunshine-brown faces from being out on the farm. All were blond, as their father, Uncle Philippe, had once been, when he had hair. All the youngest girls bounced inside, happy to be out of the rain.

Soon everyone was in dry, warm clothes, all cozy around a large stone fireplace. The whole house had a floor made from wide, smooth stones. This home was much larger than the Martineau home. In the farmhouse, they all sat in the big main room—the "fire room"—at the center and back of the house. To the front of it, sat the cooking and eating area. From both sides of the cooking area and the fire room were doors leading to two rooms on each side. Normally, the cousins would sleep on one side and the parents in the other, but now with the Martineaus here, the cousins moved to their parents' side of the house, and all the Martineaus would use the two bedrooms on the opposite side.

The rain continued to fall and cold, night winds started beating the side of the house, but inside the two families were snug and warm. Aunt Catherine had made big bowls of thick, vegetable soup for everyone, and Uncle Philippe picked out one of his choice bottles of wine to warm everyone's insides. Albret and Renée wrapped their hands around small, metal goblets. Then everyone moved into the fire room and sang some of their favorite Psalms, and both Father and Uncle Philippe prayed, giving thanks to God for His protection. Uncle Philippe had his daughter, Elizabeth, a very polite and quiet girl, play her violin, and the twins thought that these sounds were some of the most beautiful that they had ever heard. Mary missed her flute that the dragoons had taken, but she too was overwhelmed by Elizabeth's violin playing.

After a while, heavy eyelids began to droop, though it was still early. Guilliaume nodded off once and fell off the bench, mumbling, "Hot." Abraham was exhausted and slowly nodded off, with Renée and Albret already snoring lightly as they leaned against his lap. Father and Mother carried and scooted their children off for a long, warm sleep.

CHAPTER EIGHT

The Pretended Freethinker

Several weeks had passed, and though it was late September, the area was still quite warm. September and the beginning of October were the main harvest times for most vineyards. The whole farm was quite busy with workers cutting and gathering whole grape clusters from the vines. Uncle Philippe explained how harvesting a vine on just the right day was crucial for making a good wine—a little too early and the wine would be too thin, a little too late and the wine would be too strong. All around the edges of the vineyard lay large, grass mats, on which the harvested clusters would sit in the sun to perfect their ripening once off the vine itself.

Father and Abraham worked side-by-side with the other workers and Uncle Philippe in the fields. The days were long and hot, but they enjoyed this different kind of work now that the fabric shop had to be closed while the dragoons still oppressed the town.

On this day, Renée and Albret were walking through the cool, stone house, having been outside every chance they could get. Their cheeks were now more full of sunshine, just like their cousins.

"Mamá? Mamá?" they called and walked into the kitchen area to deposit some grapes for the family to use. Their eyes brightened, and they giggled when they saw Mother and Father there, kissing again and smiling. Father, with a blank face, turned his head to look at the girls and then turned back to squeeze and kiss Mother, this time dipping her backwards until they both lost their balance and almost fell over.

All four of them laughed, and then Father, with pretend anger, asked the twins, "What do you want from her? She's mine. Leave her alone." The girls giggled again and gave their grapes to Mother. She stored them in a cool place for after dinner.

A while later, Abraham came in from the fields for a moment's rest. Mother had finished Mary's Latin lesson for that day, but after Mother left, a few more questions came to Mary's mind. Abraham was also very good at Latin and had several years more practice. He sat with Mary for quite a while, helping her with her questions and giving her hints. He was very patient. It reminded him that he hoped to start college within the year.

Mother returned to the kitchen with Guilliaume and let him play with some big kitchen utensils while she started making the evening's bread. Soon Aunt Catherine joined her, and they both moved smoothly throughout the kitchen, preparing the evening meal.

Guilliaume kept getting in the way, and Mother had to smack his hands several times. Once he reached up on the counter and nearly pulled a sack of flour onto his head. Mother took him aside and scolded him sternly, smacking his hand again, and threatening greater punishment next time. The twins and the three younger cousins came in from outside and plopped down in the eating area. They just sat, watched the mothers cooking, and talked among themselves.

While Mother and Aunt Catherine were carrying something heavy off a table, Guilliaume made his move again. He just had to touch that fabric bag bulging with brown stuff. It seemed to sit there, calling for him. He walked over slowly, stood on the tips of his toes, and stretched for the flour. Before any of the girls or Mother could react to what he was doing, the bag tipped over. Flour poured onto his head and down through his robe. He was so shocked he didn't move, so the flour just kept falling, making puffy, brown clouds all around him. He desperately waved his arms in the air to somehow make it all stop.

In an instant, Mother tipped the bag back and stared at the pathetic child in anger. Flour was caked all around his wide eyes and up his nose. He had little mounds of flour piled on his outstretched palms and the top of his head. He coughed some flour out of his mouth. He hung his head down. The girls sat in disbelief. Aunt Catherine had to turn away to keep from laughing. Mother tightened her lips, too, to keep from smiling.

"'Your sin will find you out,' little man," Mother rebuked. Guilliaume knew he was in big trouble, and so he started to cry. Mother, carrying a smooth, wooden, stirring spoon, carefully marched him outside to dust off the flour and help him never forget his disobedience.

After the evening meal, everyone was tired from work that day. It was a warm evening, and Aunt Catherine opened the front and back doors to let some of the breeze come through. While they cleaned up, they heard a soft knock at the side of the front doorway.

"Good evening," said the quiet voice.

Uncle Philippe stood up to see the person and shouted, "Hello, come on in. We've been waiting for you. Look, Catherine, it's nephew Louis from Paris."

Uncle Philippe introduced Louis to everyone, and Mother pulled together a meal for him. Nephew Louis—Louis Colbert—the son of Uncle Philippe's sister in Paris, had written to Uncle Philippe some time ago, asking if he could stay for a night or two while he was traveling through.

Louis was a tall, very thin, young man with very blond hair. He had a pale, city face and soft hands. Uncle Philippe's sister was not a Christian and neither was her son Louis. He had been attending the university in Paris for several years now and thought he was very well-trained in the wisdom of the world. He had only met Uncle

Philippe and his family two other times, and those meetings were brief.

At the table, everyone crowded around Louis to hear the latest news from Paris. They wanted to know about the King's plans toward the Huguenots, but Louis did not know and was not very concerned with that news anyway. Instead, he told them of all the *new* clothes, and *new* clubs, and *new* ideas, and *new* friendships he had made with so many people. He told them of his *new* books, his *new* diary, his *new* hairstyle. Mary was polite, but she wasn't very interested in all such *newness*. It was as if Louis were from a world made up only of children, she thought.

After a while, the cousins went off to bed, as did Mary, Mother, and Aunt Catherine. But Father and Uncle Philippe continued speaking with Louis, who worried them. Abraham, who was several years younger than Louis, was also interested to listen. Father hesitated at first, but the twins also wanted to stay up. They didn't know what to make of Louis and wanted to find out more. They had forgotten about how tired they were and sat next to Abraham against the wall. Father and Uncle Philippe sat facing Louis at the table.

After Louis stopped talking so much about himself, he put a question to Father and Uncle Philippe.

"So, though you are Huguenots, you must have some favorite new thinker, don't you?"

Looking at the table, Father smiled. "I must confess, I have never been impressed with the thinking coming out of Paris. Christ is my Lord. As the Scriptures say, 'Has not God made foolish the wisdom of the world?' They are all idolaters, making up their own gods after their imaginations."

"Oh, no, no, no, no, no," chuckled Louis, "You must not have read the latest. My favorite is a thinker named La Rochefoucauld (roe-sha-foo-COE). Have you read him? He is most brilliant. He is not foolish or an idolater. Like me, he doesn't believe in any god or church or Bible. He writes brilliant sayings, such as 'We are never so happy or so unhappy as we think,' and 'We only condemn vice and praise virtue from a selfish motive,' and 'The mind is always the dupe of the heart.'"

"Why," asked Uncle Philippe, "do you think that that is not idolatry?"

"Simply," said Louis, leaning back and resting his hands behind his head, "because we have no idols. I am a freethinker—a person free from God and church."

"That's rather naive," observed Uncle Philippe. "Surely you know that you don't need statues to be an idolater. The Scriptures declare that men set up idols in their hearts. To me . . . it sounds as if you have merely substituted a false god in place of the true God."

"What nonsense," sighed Louis, "I honor no God. I am free."

Somewhat stunned, this comment made Albret think of her catechism that taught: ' . . . we clearly see that nothing worse can happen to a man than not to live to God.'

Father sat up. "Louis, you have merely set yourself up as God. That is the most common form of idolatry."

"Ah, I see," smiled Louis, "Okay, okay, in that sense, I am my own god making my own commandments for myself." He waved a hand in the air like a king and laughed nervously.

Renée sat wide-eyed, not believing that someone would say such a thing. Abraham wanted to get in on the conversation.

"But," said Father, "if you act as your own god, isn't that the worst kind of slavery? You are not a freethinker at all."

"Why," asked Louis, "would you think I am a slave for making my own commandments?"

"Well," said Father, "even your own La Rochefoucauld has written, 'Fools and simpletons judge things in terms of themselves,'" Father said raising his eyebrows, smiling.

"You know Rochefoucauld?" asked Louis.

"As I said, I wasn't impressed," said Father, "but I have read him . . . But, what do you think? Is he right? If it's true, then aren't you being foolish in setting yourself up as God? And what's more, you yourself told us that 'The mind is always the dupe of the heart.' Doesn't that make you a slave of your own foolishness? A slave of sin?"

Louis coughed a little on his drink.

"Maybe it does," he hurriedly confessed, "but

what else do I have? So, I'm a sinner. I just don't see your supposed God."

Uncle Philippe joined in, "Oh, come now, 'Men cannot open their eyes without being compelled to see God.' He has engraved unmistakable marks of His glory, so clear that no one has excuse for their disobedience."

"I think you are wrong. I cannot see God," said Louis.

"But my dear nephew, you act as if God is your judge and creator. You trust that seasons come and go. You confessed your own failings when compared to His holiness. You fear death. You use the mind He has given you. You substitute your own superstitions for Him . . . "

"And," added Father, "since your actions show your reliance upon your Creator, you know that you are His handiwork and so are owned by Him by right of creation. Therefore, shouldn't you give thanks to God for whatever you have or do? . . . And if you don't, doesn't it follow that your life is wickedly corrupt unless you honor His name and trust in Him?"

Louis sat for a long moment, looking into his glass. The girls stirred, waiting for him to speak.

Visibly bothered, Louis answered quietly, "I am traveling about trying to find the answers to such questions . . . but . . ." and he stopped.

Calmly, Uncle Philippe put his hand on Louis's shoulder, "My nephew, the wisest man tried life without God, and he concluded that, 'I have seen all the works which have been done under the sun, and behold, all is vanity and striving after the wind.' He learned that the beginning of wisdom and the fruit of life is to fear God and keep His commandments."

They all sat quietly for a while, thinking.

"I think I had better turn in for the night," said Louis.

"Yes, we all should," Uncle Philippe smiled at the twins, who were still bright-eyed.

That night in bed, Albret and Renée still couldn't sleep. They kept thinking about the discussion at the table. They didn't understand all of it, but they knew that God was good to them and thought it was horrible that someone would think he could be God for himself. That was just foolish.

CHAPTER NINE

Fruitful Lessons

Nephew Louis lingered with the families for several days longer than he had planned, watching and listening and discussing. He had never seen people living so closely and showing such kindness, sincerity, and gentleness to one another. His friends and relatives in Paris were coarsely different.

Finally, Louis continued on his journey, though he could have stayed as long as he wanted. Mother and Aunt Catherine supplied him with a big sack of fine foods, and Uncle Philippe gave him an old Bible. Then he was off. He would never forget them.

That afternoon, Mother and Mary sat, patiently teaching Renée and Albret how to sew. For the longest time, the twins had begged their mother to teach them, but sometimes their little fingers just couldn't control the needles properly. Nevertheless, with practice, they gradually got better. "Anything good requires hard work," Mother used to say.

A little later, when Aunt Catherine and her daughters joined in as well, Uncle Philippe came in and whispered a question to Mother and Aunt Catherine. In response, they agreed, nodding their heads. Uncle Philippe turned to all the girls at the table and announced, "I need some very good,

French, grape-crushing girls."

The cousins shouted in glee, but Renée and Albret weren't familiar with making wine. After making sure that their mother had given them permission, Renée and Albret followed the cousins and Uncle Philippe out to the wine-making shed. There he explained to the twins all the steps for making fine, red wine. The wine grapes had to be harvested carefully, ripened on the sunshine mats, crushed in wooden tubs and presses, and separated from their stems. Their juice had to be carefully cured with their seeds and skins, separated off, fermented in several steps, and stored in oak casks from Poland, plus many other steps that the sisters didn't really understand. But they were more than glad to do their part in the crushing.

All the girls tied their dresses up around their waists and washed their feet. They walked on wooden planks up to several wooden tubs, where some of the farmhands were already crushing and pressing grapes. The tubs were long and deep, so when everyone was ready, and a farm hand had filled the bottom of two tubs with ripened grape clusters, Uncle Philippe lifted cousin Marthe, Albret, and Renée into one tub of grapes. He placed the other cousins in a tub just next to the first. Renée and Albret hesitated as they were being set inside, and Uncle Philippe had to assure them that they would enjoy it. The cousins certainly did.

Renée felt the grapes ooze around her toes and soon started stepping up and down with large steps. Albret stood there for a moment feeling the warm clusters against her shins, and then she too started stepping up and down, squeezing out juice. Marthe and the other two cousins in the adjoining tub were already crushing grapes at full force, since they had done this many times. Renée and Albret didn't speak much but grinned at each other and raised their eyebrows in fun as they got better at it.

Uncle Philippe went to tend to other matters, and after what seemed a long while, all the girls' legs started getting tired. The cousins had made more juice and skins than Renée and Albret, but that was fine. A farmhand would put the finishing touches on the grapes where it was needed. Albret and Renée were leaning heavily against the side of the tub when Uncle Philippe returned and lifted them all out. They hadn't really looked at their legs before, but the twins marveled at the dark red color that covered their legs to just above their knees. Albret ran her finger along her leg and looked at the color on her finger. Renée ran her whole hand through the color and licked it. It didn't taste good yet. Soon the cousins showed them how to clean up and remove all the dark red from their legs and drops from their dresses.

"When can we do it again?" asked Albret.

"Soon, soon," answered Uncle Philippe. "Thank you for your help. You are now real French country girls."

"I like the squish, squish on my toes," said Renée. When they returned to the house, they excitedly sat Mother down and told her the whole story from beginning to end.

By then, it was mid-afternoon, and Aunt Catherine and Mother set out to the family garden to collect some sweet fruits for pies they wished to make. Aunt Catherine had tended this garden for many years, and it had well-supplied their family with all the fruits and vegetables they needed. It was much larger than the twins' garden had been.

Mother and Aunt Catherine stood in the sunshine, carefully picking the best plums, apricots, and other fruits from the short trees, placing the best selections in their aprons that they held out to make baskets. Some of the fresh produce would be used in the pies, and others would be stored.

Aunt Catherine took special pleasure and thanks in seeing the garden—the work of her hands—turn out well. As the two women selected their fruit, they greatly enjoyed each other's company, as they had when growing up with each other. They discussed many different topics, but being mature and godly, they never gossiped but always spoke in faith, whether discussing their children or the church or the King.

Renée and Albret saw them from a distance and wanted to join in, as they had many times before. They smiled as they walked into the garden, and since Mother and Aunt Catherine were deep in conversation, the twins knew well not to interrupt. Instead, they listened.

"I can't even imagine," answered Aunt Catherine.

"Neither can I. And that's just around here. Many more thousands have recanted their faith throughout the rest of France," said Mother.

Renée and Albret had heard of 'recanting one's faith' many times. To recant or abjure is to give up or turn away from one's faith. In the case of Huguenots it meant that one denied the biblical faith and returned to the Roman Church. At that time, the dragoons were successful in forcing many weak Huguenots into recanting their faith. Sometimes whole cities would recant as soon as the dragoons arrived in their towns.

"The Roman Church officials and the King offer great sums of money to anyone who will deny their faith. They even offer to pay off or release them from their debts for several years," added Mother.

"That is just so wicked," Aunt Catherine observed. "I've heard of some Roman Church officials boasting about how much they've paid for Huguenot conversions, especially many pastors . . . What a terrible testimony to our faith. No wonder we are mocked throughout the land. Surely, we deserve the Lord's judgment."

"Somehow—and I say this without any intention of boasting but in fear—it appears that many more men than women have recanted their faith. They must not have husbands like ours," they both laughed confidently.

"But that's why many faithful women in the

south have been forced into convents away from their children," remembered Aunt Catherine. "I don't know how I could live with myself. I know we dare not boast in our own strength, for our hearts are deceitful, but we can trust that the Lord will keep us from falling," added Aunt Catherine.

"That's my prayer. Remember Jude: 'Now to Him who is able to keep you from stumbling, and to make you stand in the presence of His glory blameless with great joy.'

"And, on top of that, how could we ever look into our children's eyes knowing that the Lord will visit our sin on them for generations," said Mother, her apron basket nearly full now. They both grew quiet for a moment, and that was Albret's cue to ask a question.

"Mamá, may I ask a question?"

"Yes, of course, my love."

"Why . . . do people re . . . re . . . "

"Recant?" asked Mother.

"Yes, why do people recant the Lord?"

"Well," Mother thought carefully, "the King is of the Roman Church, and he has decided that everyone in his land must follow his way, so he forces Huguenots to recant, thinking that he is doing a good work. Now, some Huguenots who recant later come back, and we welcome them with open arms. But others . . . if they never come back to biblical faith, then they show that they never really belonged to the Lord in the first place. As Scripture says, 'If they had been of us, they would have continued with us.'"

Renée thought about that for a moment while biting a plum. Then she asked a question.

"Mamá, how do we know if we really belong to the Lord?"

"The Lord promises us that the children of faithful parents belong to Him. He promises to be their God and to give them the Holy Spirit. So, you really belong to God." Mother smiled at them waiting for another question. Then she added, "There's another way we know that we belong to the Lord."

"What's that?" asked Albret.

"Do you see that fruit tree in the corner of the garden?" Mother pointed to a greyish, drooping tree with tiny, shriveled fruit hanging from it.

"Yes."

"What's the matter with that tree?" Mother asked.

"It looks dead," offered Renée.

"Would you like to eat some of its fruit?"

The girls both laughed, "No."

"No of course not," agreed Mother. "For some reason that little tree is sick or bad, and it can't produce any good fruit. But these good trees produce beautiful fruit. People are like that too."

Renée tilted her head for an explanation.

"Scripture tells us that God's people produce good fruit, but enemies and hypocrites produce bad fruit. So that's why we pray and ask the Lord to teach us obedience and to produce the fruit of the Spirit in us. If we see that good fruit in us, then we know that we belong to him. If we don't see it, then we should fear . . . Do you still remember the fruit of the Spirit that we learned?"

"Yes," started Albret, "the fruit of the Spirit is love, joy, peace, long-suffering, kindness—"

"And," continued Renée, "kindness, goodness, faithfulness, gentleness, and self-control."

"Very good. You remembered." They smiled.

"So, we pray that the Lord will make us full of love and peace and kindness and all the other marks of God's Spirit in us, and these show us that we belong to the Lord. But hypocrites—those just pretending to be Christians—don't show the fruit of the Spirit but show bad fruit: unfaithfulness, hatred, selfishness, contentiousness, envy, and the like. Good trees produce good fruit. Bad trees produce bad fruit."

"I want the Lord to make good fruit in me," said Albret.

"Me too," joined Renée.

"Me too," added Mother. "Now let me see the fruit you've gathered in your dresses." They held them out for Mother and Aunt Catherine to see.

"Very good. These look delightful." Mother took a suspicious step between them and the house. "Now, there's just one more thing to do," she said, taking another step backward toward the house.

"What?"

With a very serious face, Mother instructed,

"The last one to the house doesn't get any pie!"
And she ran off.

The girls squealed, and Aunt Catherine
shouted. All four of them ran clumsily, holding
their fruit in front of them.

CHAPTER TEN

Dust of Wrath

Renée thought that the morning fog seemed a little strange that Lord's Day. It hung heavily and more grey than usual. But fall changed everything. Albret fed Bouclé some vegetables, and then both twins were ready for church. Several weeks had passed, and the month of October was upon them. The vineyard harvest was coming to an end.

On this morning, when all were ready to leave for church, everyone climbed into the wagon for the trip. All the parents sat tightly together in the front seat, and all the children filled the back. They had to leave early as usual, since the horse and wagon couldn't race into town. On the way in, Albret quietly sang several psalms in her head, trying to guess which of them they might sing in worship that morning. Renée thought about the family worship the night before, when Father had taught them more about fearing and respecting God's name like Isaiah did.

By the time their wagon reached the edge of the city, most of the fog had lifted, and, from warming fireplaces, a layer of smoke hung over the city. The sun shone weakly through some high clouds. In the normal quiet of a Lord's Day morning, the parents all noticed the sound of shouting voices carrying through the air from the town.

Uncle Philippe pulled the reigns and brought the horse to a stop. Renée and Albret stood up and listened, holding on to the back of the parents' seat. For a while, no one spoke.

"It sounds like happy shouts," concluded Albret. And it did. Uncle Philippe started the horse moving again, and soon they were inside the city, moving slowly down side streets, still listening carefully. The cheering and the laughter became louder. Finally, they came around to the long street leading up to their church and, from a distance, saw the back of the cheering crowd that surrounded their church-house building.

The wagon stopped cold, and the horse whinnied nervously. Father stood and leaned forward to get a better look. All the children were standing, mouths hanging open.

At the far end of the street, their little, modest building sat in pieces. The roof had been smashed and had fallen in. Wall planks slowly fell away as stones were pulled out. Inside, all the familiar benches, tables, and psalters sat under broken wood and stones. The two families could see the destruction, but they heard no smashing, only cheers and laughter from the surrounding crowd. After a burst of dust, the whole front wall of the church teetered and then fell backward into a pile of rubble. The front of the crowd scattered for a moment and then let out another loud cheer. The dragoons who had started the demolition now started dispersing the crowd.

Father was still standing, and just then a hand

grabbed his leg and his body jumped. He instantly shook free and then realized that Elder Morin had touched him. Father jumped down from the wagon to speak with him.

Hurriedly, Elder Morin explained, "We received notice this morning from Paris that the King has revoked the last of the laws protecting Reformed Christians. He says that since so many of the Reformed have converted back to the Roman Church, he no longer needs to extend the protection once given, and now says that he wants to remove all memory of our faith from his kingdom."

Father sighed. "For years we knew this was coming. What else has the King decreed?"

Elder Morin, glanced at the rubble and the crowd and answered, "The King has banned all worship assemblies, preaching of God's word, and Reformed schools. All pastors must convert to the Roman Church or leave within fifteen days. All our children are from now on to be baptized and educated in the Roman Church on pain of penalty," Elder Morin said without wavering.

"Ha," scoffed Father with a confident grin, "the heirs of the covenant will not be forced into the idolatry of the Roman Church."

Elder Morin more than agreed. "You must return home now," said Elder Morin. "After sundown, we will meet for worship in the small forest clearing south of town, where we met in years past."

"I remember," nodded Father. Elder Morin

started to hurry off and then ran back to the wagon as it was moving off. He beckoned for Father to come to him so that he could whisper outside the hearing of the children. Father slid down again.

"You should know, brother," said Elder Morin, "that last night the dragoons emptied your fabric shop and leveled your home. You cannot return."

Father sighed and patted Elder Morin on the back, thanking him solemnly for the news. Soon the wagon was out of town heading quickly back to the farm.

Once back inside the farm house, Father and Uncle Philippe explained the King's wicked actions and calmed everyone down. From the front door, Abraham quietly watched the road for dragoons. After a long time of prayer, in which each child prayed, they remained indoors that afternoon. Albret and Renée were looking forward to holding church in the forest. They didn't know what to expect.

The families ate the evening meal early that afternoon, since the October sun set earlier and earlier each night. Quickly, they cleaned the eating area and were soon back in the wagon heading for the south side of town. The special forest clearing was closer to the farm than the town itself, so they didn't have to travel nearly as far.

As they neared the clearing, Father and Uncle Philippe stared through the trees to try and find the exact place. There were so many trees, and it had been several years since they had been there. Mother saw it first and pointed. Uncle Philippe tied the horse and wagon off the road, behind some bushy trees, and they all climbed out of the wagon.

Father carried Guilliaume and Phoebe through the trees, and Mother held the twins' hands. As they moved through the trees and brush, Mary's hair got tangled in a branch for a moment, and Albret tripped over a fallen branch, scraping her knee through her dress.

The evening temperature was still pleasant, and soon they met up with other church families gathered in the forest clearing. Pastor De Laune and his wife, Hannah, greeted them, as did Elders Morin and Pasquier. A few families were still to arrive, but in the end there was quite a big gathering. Only one family failed to show up.

Soon, far away from the ears of the city, the Huguenots began to pray and sing. Mother's other sister, Aunt Annet, and her husband and family sat on fallen logs near her other sisters and their families. Abraham was old enough to remember when they had to meet out here before. It seemed to have lasted for months, and he wondered how this time would turn out. In between Scripture readings, Renée gazed upward through the circle of towering trees and could see stars twinkling through some thin, high clouds. Those stars. She remembered what her father had told them. Someday they won't burn down our churches any more, she thought. Guilliaume flicked a small bug off his robe and rocked gently back and forth on his log-seat. At one point, Phoebe got fussy and started to cry, so Mother carried her behind the gathering, rocking her ever so gently on her shoulder.

Pastor De Laune rose and began to deliver his sermon, opening with the latest news from the La Rochelle. All the Reformed churches had been levelled to the ground. Several homes had been destroyed, and three families from other congregations had already packed and secretly moved away to Holland. One pastor had been imprisoned but was doing well, and one elder was missing.

Pastor De Laune encouraged and exhorted his people by preaching from I Peter 1:6-8: "Greatly rejoice, though now for a little while, if need be, you have been grieved by various trials, that the genuineness of your faith, being much more precious than gold that perishes, though it is tested by fire, may be found to praise, honor, and glory at the revelation of Jesus Christ, whom having not seen you love."

After only a short while into the sermon, a young man of the church came running into the gathering, breathing very hard. He was an elder's son who had been set by the road to listen for any trouble. Catching his breath, he whispered to the Pastor.

"Pastor De Laune . . . the dragoons . . . twenty or so . . . are coming . . . this way! They are yet . . . over . . . the hill," he gasped.

"Very well," stiffened the Pastor, "Brothers and sisters, there is a time to stand and a time to hide. The dragoons are upon us. Hide in the forest to the west and the south. Return to your homes later or in the morning. God be with you!"

Without a word, fathers and older brothers picked up smaller children and set off into the forest. Father picked up the twins, Abraham grabbed Guilliaume and Phoebe, and Mother and Mary ran holding hands. Uncle Philippe picked up Marthe and Sarah, and Aunt Catherine lifted Jeanette and held Elizabeth's hand alongside her. They all could hear the horses and clinking of the soldiers. But Pastor De Laune, his wife, and two children stood firm.

Father and Uncle Philippe paused to listen and offer help, and the two elders spoke hurriedly to the Pastor.

"—but you must go. You will be imprisoned if you stay," stressed Elder Pasquier.

With a quick, authoritative whisper, Pastor De Laune declared to both elders, "'But a hireling who is not the shepherd, one who does not own the sheep, sees the wolf coming and flees; and the wolf catches the sheep and scatters them.' I am not a hireling. Please brethren, take my wife and children and go now."

Elder Pasquier, in exasperation, turned to the Pastor's wife, "Dear Hannah, please plead for your husband's life. Persuade him to leave. He may be separated from you and your children forever."

Hannah gently touched the elder's cheek and

smiled. "He is a faithful watchman, called and under duty to Christ to protect these sheep. I would expect nothing less from him."

"You see," added the Pastor, "I may fail like Adam, but my wife is no Eve. Go now, I will keep the dragoons' attention here. Care for my wife and children, if need be." After a quick embrace of her husband, Hannah and all the others ran into the forest.

No one looked back at the Pastor, but if they had, they would have seen him calling the dragoons over to himself.

"Over here, over here. I am the one you want," he called out. When they finally heard him, all the dragoons stopped looking elsewhere and surrounded Pastor De Laune. They stared down at him from their tall horses. He started asking the dragoons questions about their authority and the King's recent changes, all to give his people more time to flee. Finally, the captain angrily stopped answering questions.

"Will you deny that you assembled your people here for religious exercises of the pretended reformed religion, though you know that the King has forbidden all such assemblies?" asked the dragoon captain.

Looking the captain straight in the eye, Pastor De Laune spoke slowly and calmly, still delaying as much as possible, "I will most forthrightly confess that I called such an assembly and that in these circumstances I am bound, as were the Holy Apostles, to obey God rather than man and that . . ." The dragoon kicked him in the chest, knocking him to the ground.

"Tie him to my horse. I will drag him to jail," he ordered one dragoon. He ordered the others to pursue any people fleeing through the forests. The soldiers rode off, though because of the thickness of the trees, their horses couldn't get very far, as the elders knew. So the dragoons dismounted and started running through the forest on foot.

The remaining soldier bound Pastor De Laune's legs together and then ran a rope from them to the captain's saddle. The captain rode off dragging the praying Pastor behind him. The captain was pleased that he had captured another pastor; he would be rewarded for this. No one ever saw Pastor De Laune again.

Father, Uncle Philippe, and Abraham grew more tired as they ran, carrying the children. Abraham kept looking back, and Phoebe cried loudly. Father held the twins firmly against his chest. They buried their faces in his shirt, since so many branches kept scratching them. Once, Father tripped, and all three of them fell into some thorny bushes.

Though the believers kept running and hiding, the dragoons had long given up searching. Pastor De Laune had delayed the soldiers so long that not one dragoon came even close to any of the families.

Finally, all the wives and children gathered around the fathers, and though a few people had small cuts, scratches, and bruises, no one was seriously hurt. Uncle Philippe's family met up with the Martineaus, and they decided to spend the night in the forest, since they were far from the wagon and the farm. Father and Abraham cleared away some underbrush, and Uncle Philippe, Elizabeth, and Mary gathered piles of soft leaves to sleep on.

Though the temperature was still pleasant, all the children snuggled closely to their parents. Father asked Mother to pray, thanking the Lord for protecting them, hoping that He would protect Pastor De Laune. Mother and Aunt Catherine planned to visit the Pastor the next day in jail, but he wouldn't be there. Renée and Albret asked their parents to sing them to sleep with a psalm. With all the children huddled together, Father and Mother quietly sang, until all the tired, little eyes had closed:

> Secured by thine unfailing grace, In thee they
>   find a hiding place.
> When foes their plots devise; A sure retreat
> thou
>   wilt prepare
> And keep them safely sheltered there . . .

CHAPTER ELEVEN

Anchor of Faith

The midday sun shone brightly over the harvested vineyards, and Renée and Albret sat quietly, feeding Bouclé in the shade by the back door of the farm house. They watched Father and Mother holding hands and walking through a field, discussing something very serious, the twins guessed.

The two families had been back at the farm for two days after their night in the forest. They had found their wagon still intact and driven it back to the farm. Mother, Father, Uncle Philippe, and Aunt Catherine had been speaking among themselves quite often since that night. Father and Uncle Philippe had also traveled to town the previous day to meet with the elders. Among other things, they learned that the family that didn't show up for worship in the forest that night had abandoned their faith when threatened by the dragoons and had rejoined the idolatrous, Roman Church. They had also told the dragoons where the worship service was to be held.

When Father and Uncle Philippe returned the previous day, the twins asked about Pastor De Laune.

"Did you see Pastor De Laune in the prison?" asked Albret.

Father pulled his girls beside him as he sat on

a bench in the fire room. Others in the family listened in as well.

Father asked the twins, "Do you understand what Pastor De Laune did for all the church people?"

The girls stared and thought.

Father continued, "He did a very brave and faithful thing for all of us. While we were running, he slowed the soldiers. He made them talk to him so that we could get safely away . . . But in the end, the dragoons took him away."

"To prison?" asked Renée anxiously.

"No. He's not in prison, and no one knows where he is."

Albret looked down. Renée bit her lip gently. They loved and respected Pastor De Laune very much.

"Wherever he is," explained Father, "we should all understand his example. The Lord Jesus says that no man shows a greater love for his friends than when he lays down his life for them. Pastor De Laune was willing to do that for the people set under his care. You know that the Lord Jesus died in the place of His people, as a substitute so that we could live. In a lesser way, Pastor De Laune may have stood in our place too, taking the anger and punishment of the dragoons so that we could get away. Christ loves His people, and Pastor De Laune learned from Jesus' example."

"Will we ever see Pastor De Laune again?" asked Renée.

Father now looked down. "I don't think so.

Not here on earth at least. But we will surely be with him again in heaven."

The twins put their heads in Father's lap and cried silently.

The girls remembered that discussion as they sat watching Father and Mother walking in the vineyard. They saw Uncle Philippe walk out to speak to Father and Mother, and after a few moments of talking, the parents nodded their heads, and Uncle Philippe, looking pleased, started back toward the barn.

That night after the evening meal, the girls and all the children learned of the decision that the parents had reached. It was at once frightening and sad, but also exciting. Father and Uncle Philippe explained to the children that the King had forbidden Huguenots to assemble for worship and demanded that all Huguenot children be taught by teachers in the Roman Church, but, of course, no faithful Christian parents would let their children be taught by idolaters. The dragoons were threatening and beating many Huguenots into converting to the idolatrous, Roman Church, and it didn't look like any of this would stop as it had in years before.

So, after much prayer and discussion, they had decided that it was now time for both families to leave France and settle in England. Other Huguenots had left for Holland, Switzerland, Brandenburg (now Germany), Carolina, and even Africa. In the end, over three thousand Huguenots would flee from La Rochelle. But there was still a problem. For several years the King had forbidden Huguenots to leave France, instead forcing them to remain and face the dragoons. Nevertheless, Uncle Philippe had arranged with a friend for a ship to meet them and take them to England, but they had to leave secretly the following evening.

The children had many questions, mainly about England and what it was like. They were all very excited. It seemed like an adventure. But they were reminded that it would be dangerous and that all the children must do exactly as they were told at every moment, without questions. Everyone would have to be strong. And after saying that, Father turned to Renée and Albret, and as gently as he could, he told them that Bouclé would have to stay here. Uncle Philippe had a farmhand who had agreed to take very good care of Bouclé and keep him as a pet. A few more tears fell. Father wiped them away and reminded them that the Lord promised that someday, He would wipe away all His people's tears.

When the next evening came and everyone was loaded into the wagon and ready to go, Uncle Philippe stood staring at his farm one last time. He would probably never see it again. He had so enjoyed serving the Lord as a farmer and winemaker for so many years, but he knew that the Lord had something else for him to do now. He shook hands with the man who had been his chief farmhand and was now owner of the farm. Though not a Huguenot, the man was very decent and a good farmer.

Once Uncle Philippe climbed aboard, another farmhand drove the wagon and horse down the road. This farmhand would drop them off several miles down the road nearer the beach, but they couldn't take the wagon all the way since there was no connecting road to the secret place where the boat was waiting.

Knowing that they would have to walk far and have little space in the small boat, the two families took very few things with them, even less than the Martineaus had brought from town. Soon the wagon dropped them off, and everyone thanked the farmhand. Uncle Philippe patted his horse goodbye, and they all started through an open field. A large moon loomed overhead, staring down at them.

The twins didn't carry anything, because Father knew that he would probably have to carry them later on. For the moment, Father carried Guilliaume, whose legs were still too short to keep up on his own.

As the time dragged on, the terrain changed. First, they passed through grassy fields and then slight hills. Nearer the city, they had to slog through wide mud and salt flats that seemed to last forever. It would have been much easier to pass through La Rochelle and then down the coast, but they would have been seen. After several hours of slow walking, they stood behind a low grassy hill, just beyond which sat the ocean and their

boat to England. Actually, this would be the first
of two boats. This first smaller boat would take
them out to a second larger boat anchored off-
shore, and in that larger boat, they would travel
up the coast and cross over to England.

Uncle Philippe and Father went to check on
the boat, and they could see it and its owner farther down the beach. But as they walked south
toward the small boat, they heard the now familiar noises of a band of dragoons coming in
their direction from the north. Father and Uncle
Philippe were too far away to be seen by the dragoons at that moment, and they quickly hid themselves behind another grassy mound. The dragoons passed by, and Mother and Aunt Catherine
worried for their husbands, but Father and Uncle
Philippe were safe.

The soldiers rode up to the man waiting at
the boat and spoke to him for a while, but it was
too far away for Father or Uncle Philippe to hear.
As they watched, they saw the dragoons force
the man into his boat and out to sea. When the
man was far out toward his larger boat, the dragoons continued down the beach. Father and
Uncle Philippe watched in shock as their boat to
freedom moved farther and farther away. There
was nothing they could do. Uncle Philippe sat
with his face in his hands, wondering what to do
now. Father and Uncle Philippe rejoined their
families, and they all waited for another long while,
hoping that the man would return in his boat,
but Uncle Philippe knew that the man wasn't prin-

cipled and wouldn't risk losing his boats by dis-
obeying the dragoons. Uncle Philippe would have
to arrange another meeting for another day. Since
they didn't know how or when another trip could
be arranged, they would have to return to the
farm.

The trip back took much longer than the trip
there, since all of the smaller children, including
Renée and Albret, nearly fell asleep as they walked.
All the parents, and Abraham, Mary, and Elizabeth took turns carrying children, but only Phoebe
was a light carrying size, so the smaller children
shifted from walking to sleeping and back, all the
way to the farm. It was nearly sunrise when they
arrived, and the new farm owner greeted them
and cared for them well, but was sad for their
sakes.

Over the next few days Uncle Philippe and
Father kept praying and trying to arrange for another boat, but most of the boat owners were
too scared, since the King's navy was regularly
capturing boats of Huguenots at sea and taking
the boats for themselves. Other boat captains were
known for taking Huguenots out to sea and then
robbing them of all their savings and throwing
them overboard.

Finally, Father and Uncle Philippe hired a boat
captain and his boat for a very stiff price, paid
up front, though they might run into the same
problems on the beach as before. To guard against
having to return to the farm, they also contacted
an old business friend who owned a small fishing

cottage south of the meeting point, but much
closer than the farm. He agreed to let them stay
with him, if need be.

After a few days, they again loaded into the
wagon, said goodbye to the farm and Bouclé again,
and started off. The evening was colder this time,
as they made their way through the grassy hills
and crossed the wide mud and salt flats. When in
open areas, they would softly sang their favorite
psalms, which encouraged them greatly.

After several hours, they huddled near the
beach as before, though farther south for this
meeting. Father and Uncle Philippe stepped out
to search for the boat and dragoons, but they
saw neither. After a few moments, the boat captain, a Monsieur Perin, met them. He had wisely
hid his very small rowboat behind a hill so as not
to draw any attention from the dragoons. But
the boat was so small that they would need to
make two trips out to his larger boat. They decided to go by families, with the Martineaus going first.

Everyone kept praying for success and watching for dragoons, but the soldiers must have been
occupied in some other evil that night. Soon both
families had been rowed out to the larger boat.
Renée and Albret were wide awake now, for they
had never been on a boat before. They wanted
to stand tall and watch everything, but the ocean
wind was too cold. Instead, they all huddled under old, smelly sails and blankets, as the large boat

made its way past the islands just off the coast of La Rochelle.

The trip lasted longer than usual, since during the following day, they came close to several of the King's boats. When they did, the boat captain, Monsieur Perin, would stop sailing, cover up the two families, and pretend to fix or fish from the boat. The wind was constant, and this made for a bouncing sea and several seasick children. But everyone agreed that it was far better to struggle with the wind than with dragoons, who were farther and farther away with every gust.

After sailing two evenings and an early morning, they finally caught a glimpse of the English coast bathed in morning sunlight, and this gave everyone new strength. Albret wanted so badly to be able to run her hand through the water, and Renée wanted to catch a sea gull. Guilliaume just wanted to stop being sick. He would hold his stomach, mumbling, "Hot . . . hot." If they weren't sick, they were hungry. No one had eaten for over a day and a half.

The sun was rising on their right through fog, as they passed the Isle of Wight and sailed into the English harbor of Southampton, one of the larger and more important cities on the south coast of England. After another long while, they sailed into the harbor of Southampton proper and glided to a dock. They gazed at all the passing buildings made of round, grey stones. The boat's captain helped everyone onto the dock, but their legs were quite wobbly from sitting and rocking in the waves for so long. Aunt Catherine stumbled on the edge of the boat, but Uncle Philippe grabbed her firmly.

Renée and Albret waited on the thick, wooden dock, smiling at their Mother, as Abraham and Mary peered through the cool, morning fog at the waking city. This would now be home. Uncle Philippe ran ahead to find his Huguenot friend who had promised to give them lodging and introduce them to the other Huguenots already living, working, and worshipping in Southampton.

As the families walked out of the harbor, Father stepped down below the dock where it met the central market area. He was picking something up, but no one could see exactly what. When Father came back onto the dock, he went over to the twins and told them to hold out their hands and open their palms. They did. Onto their open palms, he poured two handfuls of sand. They giggled as it fell over their skin. They remembered.

He smiled at them and said, "The Lord is indeed merciful."

CHAPTER TWELVE

New Sand

Guilliaume sat on the cool, Southampton beach, gathering, piling, and pushing sand into some special shape that only he understood. He pressed white seashells into the side of the mysterious lump of sand for decoration. Never far away, Albret and Renée walked slowly up the beach toward him. Holding hands, they stared at Guilliaume's work for a while.

"What is it, Gee Gee?" asked Albret.

"Is it a castle?" asked Renée.

Looking a little upset, Guilliaume frowned and molded one part of the sand lump, adjusting its shells. Then he looked at them, as if that shift would make his work very obvious.

"I'm sorry," said Albret, "I still don't know what it is."

"It's a . . . bir . . . cow isn't it?" tried Renée, grimacing in fear of guessing incorrectly again.

"ffroomudee bellagay," he insisted angrily, and walked off in a huff.

Not having the least idea what he was talking about, the girls just stared at each other and held back a giggle. They stood and watched as Guilliaume headed back to the Martineau's cottage.

"What's a ffrum . . . oodee . . . billogee?" Albret giggled to her sister.

"If you tilt your head this way and squint your eyes," suggested Renée, "then you can clearly see that it's a sheepdog covered with tall trees." With that, they too headed back up to the cottage.

Spring was now upon Southampton, which had been home for the Martineaus for over six months. The cold, English winter, which they weren't at all used to, had gripped the city and all its Huguenot refugees for several long months. But they had all come through with only minor illnesses.

Soon after they arrived, Father and Uncle Philippe had opened a silk shop in the center of town. Though a farmer at heart, Uncle Philippe had discovered that the farmland in south England was very different than La Rochelle. So he had quickly adapted his skills to the fabric trade. Since Southampton served as one of the prime harbors for English trade, Father and Uncle Philippe had been able to send out their work to places all around the world, though the English government seemed to have almost as many rigid trade rules as the French government.

Uncle Philippe, Aunt Catherine, and all their children lived a short way from the Martineau's cottage. The local Huguenot refugees had all helped the two families get set up and started almost immediately upon arrival. As well, the residents of Southampton were known for their special kindness to the Huguenots. Long before, the residents of Southampton had provided Huguenots with a place to worship at St. Julian's Chapel, a part of an old and beautiful building known as God's House Tower which overlooked the harbor.

Mother, Aunt Catherine, and Mary did the best at learning English, though everyone followed suit, except Guilliaume, and of course, Phoebe. Because of Mary's skill at English, she often helped out in the fabric store and was well-liked by all the customers. During one of the colder parts of the winter, after a particularly good week of trading silk, Father brought home a package for Mary. He said that he had sat through too many evenings without the sound of Mary's beautiful music. When Mary opened the package, expecting a flute, she instead found a beautiful violin. She almost fainted. And soon thereafter, she was regularly by her cousin Elizabeth's side learning as much as she could. Elizabeth had left her violin behind at the farm house, but Uncle Philippe had brought home a package for her the same night Mary received hers.

From the very beginning, Abraham worked diligently at the fabric shop, learning even more and getting better at his trade. But he still wanted to study at a university. And after many encouraging discussions with Father and the elders in Southampton, Abraham desired to pursue the ministry and work toward serving as a pastor. He was well aware of many of the difficulties that the ministry promised, but his heart burned to serve in the Church. He remembered and was ashamed at so many of the Huguenot pastors that had so easily recanted their faith. The Church needed more faithful teachers, like Pastor De Laune. So, the family planned to have Abraham continue working through the year at the fabric shop, and then they would send him to study for the ministry at the French university in Edinburgh, Scotland. He could hardly wait.

Mother was busier than ever. At the beginning of winter, she took in several young, French girls from among the church families and began tutoring them in music, Latin, writing, and sewing. They had to stop for several months, because the weather was too cold and the Martineau cottage was outside of town. But now that spring had arrived, the families wanted their girls to return to their studies under Madame Martineau. This time, Renée and Albret would join in on the lessons as well, something they had long begged to do.

Renée and Albret liked any season of the year, making the best out of any climate. But spring held a special place in their hearts, as it does for many people. No sooner had they arrived at Southampton than they had been forced to remain indoors most of the time, due to the winter. They had not had any time to explore the area around their cottage. But now with spring beginning, they spent most of their days looking for seashells, examining sea creatures, and watching waves. They had quite a collection of seashells and had adorned Mother with probably a chest full of seashell necklaces.

Best of all, Father had cleared an area along the side of the cottage, where the twins could plant and tend a garden of their own. Since the climate was so different, the garden would have to be different too. They would have to learn about the vegetables and fruits that did well in the Southampton climate, which had much less sunshine than La Rochelle. Mother asked some of the Huguenot ladies from the church, who had raised several gardens of their own, to come over and explain the differences between gardens in England and those in France. The girls learned quickly, and soon they had planted all types of fruits and vegetables. Some of these they had never known before, so they couldn't wait to see what the seeds produced.

After Renée and Albret left Guilliaume's sand lump and returned to the cottage, they played with Phoebe for a while, who was now able to sit up by herself and lean against furniture. Aunt Catherine had come over with all her daughters for English tea time, a new custom for these women of La Rochelle. Mother had made delicious pastries for everyone.

After tea, Father came home and peeked his head into the house. He checked to see whether Renée and Albret were inside, and when he spotted them, he told them to wait there. Everyone listened in silence, wondering what Father was up to. They could hear two voices outside the thick house walls; perhaps they were those of Father and Uncle Philippe.

Finally, the cottage door creaked open again. Father stood there for a moment with his arms crossed, just looking at everyone. Mother smiled at this.

"You two," said Father, sternly pointing at Renée and Albret, "come outside."

Everyone got up and followed, bunching up at the top of the front door step. The twins stared at Father waiting for something, but he just stood there with his back to the waves in the distance.

"Well, do you hear?" he asked them.

"Waves?" guessed Albret.

"No."

"The city?" guessed Renée.

"No. Listen."

They stepped down from the doorway toward Father, but still they could hear nothing special. Then ever so lightly, they did start to hear a different sound. *Crunch. Crunch. Crunch.* Where had they heard that sound before? *Crunch. Crunch. Crunch.* Then they remembered. They ran around the side of the house, and there in the middle of each of their gardens, tied to two pegs, stood two, wobbly, midnight-black lambs. They were chewing on a little pile of vegetables that Father had brought from town.

"Oh Father! oh Father!" the twins yelled.

"These are the best gifts," cried Albret.

"Thank you so much," said Renée squeezing her lamb around its neck. All the other children ran over to pet the new additions to the Martineau family. After a few moments, Renée and Albret ran over to Father, who was standing in the beach sand next to Mother, holding her hand, talking. The twins hugged their parents' legs. Then Renee motioned for Father to bend over so she could say something.

"We remember the sand, Father," Renée said quietly.

"We always will," said Albret.

Father smiled deeply, and hugging them again said, "The Lord has been very gracious to us all."

Amanda Renée

At first we thought you'd never talk, you hid
so long behind moon cheeks; across our room
you rolled in twirling curls of brown. Then did
you Edmund's, Curdy's, Laura's minds assume.
Though 'gators fear and tame sparks too, you still
bike hard and tackle Mac. But best of all
you dance with sister, sing me hymns, and tell
of queens and catechism. When you're tall
and full of faith, tell stories to the world.
Seek joy and peace and faithfulness; be glad
and grateful as you watch your life unfurl,
and never live too far from old, gray Dad.
    Oh Lord, please overcome my sins and mold
    her high and holy service in Your fold.

Chelsea Albret

Upon first light you would not breathe, but grace
prevailed. Hair, too, you did withhold and hate
on monster dogs and prickling round man's face,
but love to Polka, dress-up friends in spate.
Now tea soirées and paperdoll piles fill
your social hours; you craft plots zestfully
and try your math in French and joke until
we laugh. You query me on Trinity
and Christ: so later when in faith you stand
a woman, write for Him for all to see,
teach your children all of Abram's sand,
and visit, warm me with your poetry.
    Lord, she is Yours, and You are hers in heart.
    Please make her mighty in her priestly part.

Bibliography

Aries, Philippe, *Centuries of Childhood: A Social History of Family Life* Baldick, Robert, ed., tr., (New York, NY: Alfred A. Kopf, 1962).

Calvin, John, *Selected Works of John Calvin* Beveridge, Henry, ed., tr., (Grand Rapids, MI: Baker Book House Co., [1849] 1983).

Clark, John G., *La Rochelle and the Atlantic Economy During the Eighteenth Century* (Baltimore, MD: Johns Hopkins Press, 1981).

De Mause, LLoyd, ed., *The History of Childhood* (New York, NY: Harper Torchbook, 1974).

Fontaine, James, *Memoirs of a Huguenot Family* Ann Maury, ed., tr., (Baltimore, MD: Genealogical Publishing Co. [1853] 1967).

Glenn Gray, Janet, *The French Huguenots: Anatomy of Courage* (Grand Rapids, MI: Baker Book House, 1981).

Gwynn, Robin, *Huguenot Heritage: The History and Contribution of the Huguenots in Britain* (London: Routledge and Kegan Paul, 1985).

La Brousse, Elizabeth, "Calvinism in France, 1598-1685," in Prestwich, Menna *International Calvinism 1541-1715* (Oxford: Clarendon Press, 1985).

La Rochefoucauld, Francois, *The Maxims of La Rochefoucauld* Kronenberger, Louis, tr., (New York, NY: Random House, 1959).

Joutard, Philippe, "The Revocation of the Edict of Nantes: End or Renewal of French Calvinism," in Prestwich, Menna *International Calvinism 1541-1715* (Oxford: Clarendon Press, 1985).

Mandrou, Robert, *Introduction to Modern France* Hallmark, R.E., ed., tr., (New York, NY: Holmes and Meier, 1975).

Mourgues, Odette, *Two French Moralists: La Rochefoucauld and La Bruyre* (Cambridge: Cambridge Univ. Press, 1978).

Ozment, Steven, *When Fathers Ruled: Family Life in Reformation Europe* (Cambridge, MA: Harvard Univ. Press, 1983).

Parker, David, *La Rochelle and the French Monarchy: Conflict and Order in Seventeenth-Century France* (London: Royal Historical Society, 1980).

Patterson, A. Temple, *Southampton: A Biography* (London: Macmillan & Co. Ltd., 1970).
